SAVAGE
ROGUE

A NICOLE BERETTI THRILLER

LUKA T. JACOBS

Cover Design, Book Design & Formatting: Luka T. Jacobs.

Copyright © 2024 Luka T. Jacobs. All rights reserved. No portion of this book may be reproduced in any form without written permission from the publisher or author, except as permitted by U.S. copyright law.

ISBN: 978-1-7637809-2-7

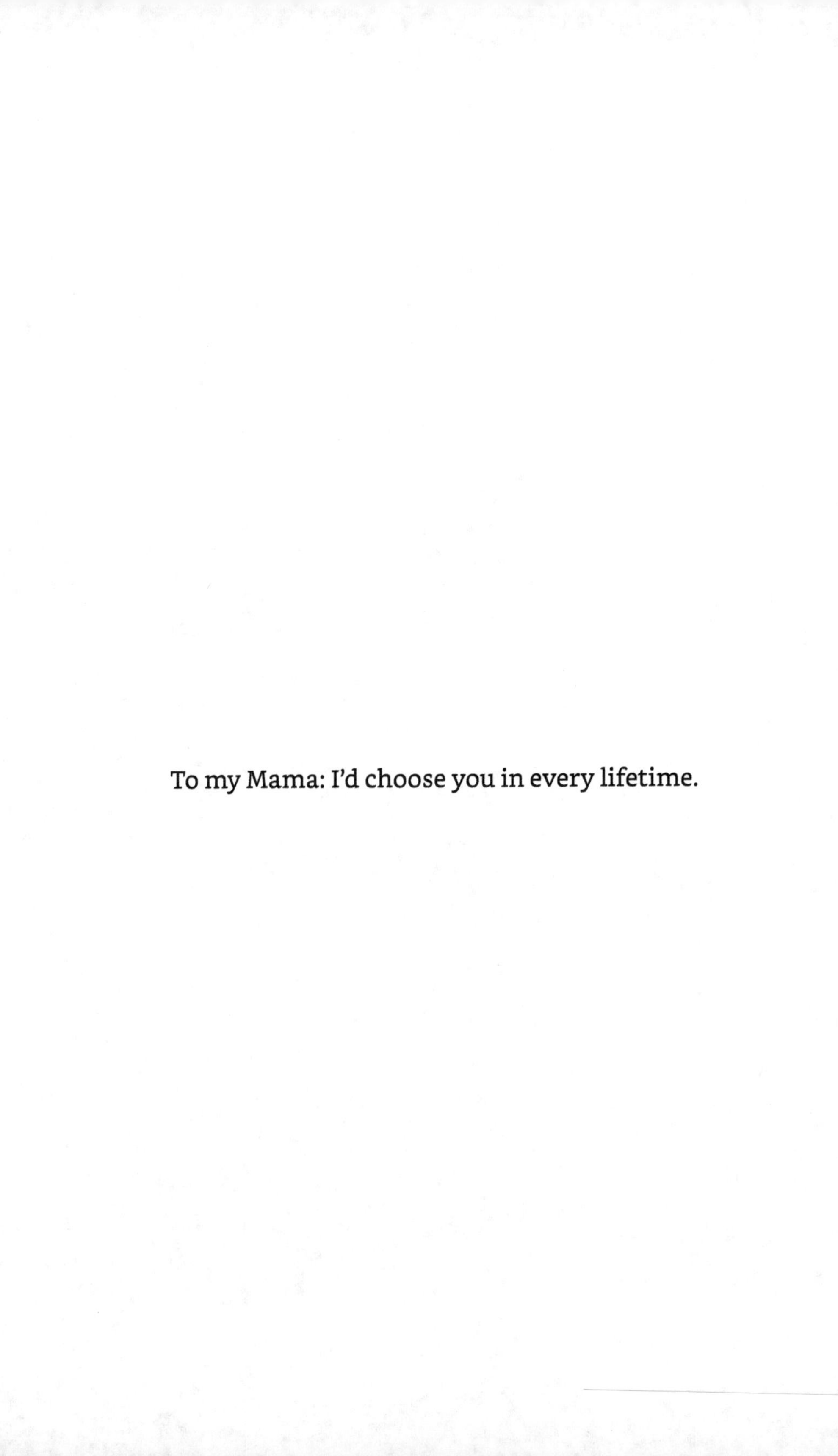

To my Mama: I'd choose you in every lifetime.

NOTE FROM THE AUTHOR

 Thank you for selecting my book as your next read! After making her debut in the third instalment of the **_Night of the Dogman_** series, **Special Agent Nicole Beretti** is back, taking the lead in her first stand-alone thriller, _Savage Rogue_. I'm excited for you to dive into this new adventure with her, and I hope you enjoy every page.

Thank you again for your support, and happy reading!

Luka T. Jacobs

Facebook: https://www.facebook.com/lukatjacobs

Amazon: https://amazon.com/author/lukatjacobs

Website: http://www.LukaTJacobs.com

CONTENTS

PROLOGUE

Crack.

A sharp snap echoed through the dense Wyoming underbrush, but Tucker and Bo barely registered it as they trudged forward, their boots sinking into the damp forest floor. Shotguns hung from their shoulders, swinging slightly with each step as they moved in tandem. The sun's first light crept slowly over the horizon, slicing through the thick morning fog that clung low to the ground, casting an eerie glow over the wilderness.

Both men, rugged and in their early thirties, were marked by a long history of poor decisions and run-ins with the law. This morning was no different. They'd spent months running an illegal trapping operation, specifically targeting grizzly bears for their lucrative pelts. Their greed dulled any caution they might have felt about their scheme's dangers. The payday was all that mattered—enough to keep them going, no matter the risk or the rules they had to break.

"Man, I'm telling ya, this is it. If we succeed in trapping another grizzly, we'll be all set for the whole winter," Bo exclaimed, his voice hoarse from years of tobacco addiction. He hocked a loogie onto the dirt and fixed his grimy baseball hat.

"It better be worth it, that's all I'm saying. Ain't no way I'm freezin' my ass off for nothin'," Tucker grumbled, pulling his jacket tighter against the cold. He was thinner and shorter than Bo, his eyes darting nervously around the forest, always on the lookout. He knew they'd be in trouble if the game wardens caught them.

A few days ago, they set up a large bear trap hidden in the forest. Made of heavy-duty steel, the contraption was designed to trap anything that ventured onto the game trails. Bo purchased it from a dubious out-of-state source, boasting that no creature could escape once its jaws closed.

"Damn thing's strong enough to catch a tank," Bo had said when they set it. "Ain't no bear getting outta this one."

The trap had been carefully set along a narrow game trail, hidden just off a small clearing where animals often ventured through. They'd chosen the location to catch an unsuspecting grizzly on its routine path, banking on the season's chill to drive it along established trails. The payout for a full bear hide, they figured, would be worth all the freezing mornings—and the constant fear of getting nabbed by Fish and Game wardens.

Tucker kicked at a patch of dirt as they neared the clearing where the trap was set. "Think we got one?"

"If we did, it ain't goin' nowhere. This trap'll hold," Bo said, slapping Tucker on the back.

As they entered the clearing, both men suddenly stopped. Something big was caught in the trap.

"What the hell...?" Tucker muttered, squinting through the misty dawn light.

A huge creature, bigger than any bear they had ever witnessed, lay partially slouched on the forest ground. At first glance, they thought it might be a wolf, but as their eyes adjusted, it was clear this was no ordinary wolf. The creature was massive, measuring well over six feet in length, covered in thick, tangled fur, and possessed a formidable physique that resembled a creature from a nightmare rather than a real animal.

Its leg was ensnared in the steel jaws of the bear trap, the metal teeth piercing flesh and fur. The ground around the trap was covered in blood, dark and sticky in the faint light, and the soil indicated a struggle had occurred. The beast had clearly fought to free itself. The ground around the trap was churned up, deep claw imprints etched into the earth where the creature had thrashed and tried to escape.

"Holy hell..." Bo whispered, stepping forward cautiously. "We... we got somethin' big. The boss is gonna love it!"

Tucker's stomach churned at the sight. "I-Is it... is it d-dead?"

Bo grinned. "Sure looks like it.

"Look at the trap," Tucker said, his voice trembling slightly. "Thing put up one hell of a fight."

Bo chuckled and approached the creature without hesitation. "Thing's as good as dead. Hell, it ain't movin' at all." He stood right next to its side, eyes gleaming with greed, and gave it a sharp kick to the ribs.

Tucker squinted, feeling a pit form in his stomach as he

took in the massive, slumped form on the ground. "What... what the hell is that?"

Bo chuckled and stepped forward without hesitation. "This, my friend, is one huge freakin' wolf. The boss is gonna pay us big-time for this." His eyes lit up as he admired the creature's massive limbs and thick fur. "I woke up with a good feeling about today."

Tucker hesitated, casting a wary glance left and right, his nerves prickling as he took in the creature's massive form. "That... that ain't a normal wolf, Bo. It's too big. Looks like a freakin' werewolf or somethin'." His voice dropped to a whisper. "Maybe we should just leave it. Somethin' about this don't feel right, I tell ya."

Bo laughed, brushing off Tucker's concern. "What are you scared of, Tuck? This thing's our payday, and it's not even breathin'." He nudged the creature's side with his boot, his grin widening. "It's dead, see?"

Tucker's gut twisted, but he stayed silent, glancing around the clearing. The thick mist clung to the air, as the hairs on his neck bristled. "Alright... let's make it quick," he muttered, looking away from the creature's enormous form.

Bo knelt down beside the trap, his fingers fumbling with

the latch. "Tucker, give me a hand with this," he muttered. Together, they pried the trap open, and with a metallic click, the jaws sprang apart, freeing the creature's leg.

For a moment, silence hung heavy in the air.

Then, in a sudden, terrifying blur, something exploded from the shadows—a dark, hulking figure hurtling out of the trees with the speed and force of a freight train. Tucker barely registered what was happening before the creature was upon them, claws flashing in the dim light.

Bo's scream was short-lived as the creature's claws tore through his side, ripping through muscle and bone with ease. Blood sprayed across the clearing, splattering Tucker's face as he stumbled back, frozen in horror. Bo's eyes widened in shock, his hands clutching at the gaping wound in his chest as he staggered, his mouth opening in a silent scream.

The creature didn't hesitate. It lunged at Bo, driving him to the ground with bone-crushing force, its jaws closing around his throat. With a sickening crunch, its teeth tore through flesh, tendons, and muscle, severing his spinal column in a single, brutal motion. Blood pooled beneath him, soaking into the dirt as his body went still, his lifeless eyes fixed on the misty sky above.

"Oh, God… oh, Jesus Christ!" Tucker stammered, his body shaking as he stumbled backward, his gaze locked on the creature that now turned its attention toward him.

The beast loomed, massive and unnatural, its muzzle dripping with blood. beneath its dense fur as it stood there, staring down at Bo's mangled body with eyes that burned with a terrifying, almost human rage.

Tucker stared, transfixed, as it rose slowly onto two legs, towering over him, its broad shoulders heaving with every breath. The creature's eyes locked onto him with a chilling, almost human rage, sharp and intelligent, gleaming with a hunger that turned his blood to ice.

Tucker felt the scream clawing its way up his throat, his mind urging him to run, but his legs were leaden, frozen by terror. The shotgun strapped across his shoulder was all but forgotten, dead weight in the haze of fear clouding his mind.

Then, with a low, guttural growl that reverberated in his chest, the beast lunged, closing the distance in a heartbeat. Its jaws clamped down on his arm, bone crunching beneath the brutal force, and in a single, terrifying wrench, it tore his arm clean off. A white-hot pain exploded through him as his scream shattered the morning silence, echoing through the trees while blood sprayed from the wound, painting the forest floor.

Tucker staggered backward, clutching at the raw, bleeding stump, his vision blurring as his strength ebbed with every heartbeat. His breaths came in shallow, panicked gasps as he stumbled through the underbrush, leaving a crimson trail in his wake.

But the beast wasn't finished.

With frightening speed, it lunged again, slashing at his legs with its powerful claws. Tucker crashed to the ground, his body convulsing in agony as blood poured from the gashes. His vision darkened at the edges, the world spinning as he struggled to breathe, his strength fading.

The creature stood over him, its gaze unwavering as it watched his life ebb away. Tucker's last, desperate attempt to crawl away was met with a swift, brutal bite, severing his leg in one savage twist. The pain was blinding, his mind barely able to comprehend the extent of his injuries as he lay helpless, his blood seeping into the earth.

With one final, ragged breath, Tucker went still, his body slumping in the grass as the life drained from him.

The creature remained for a moment, breathing heavily, its body tense as it surveyed the bloody remains of the two humans who had caused his sister's death. For a brief moment, its gaze softened as it turned back toward the lifeless form of its sibling, lying still and broken on the forest floor.

As the creature drew near, it moved with a haunting grace, dropping to all fours and lowering its massive head to nuzzle her gently, emitting a soft, mournful whine. It lingered beside her, its fury momentarily softened by a sorrow that settled deep within its chest.

Then, with one last, lingering look at the clearing, it turned and melted back into the woods, disappearing into the dense underbrush. The mist closed around it, swallowing its form as it silently left the clearing behind.

ONE

The following morning dawned in muted grays, light filtering weakly through low clouds as the creature lay motionless by the creek. Cold water numbed his paws, a welcome relief from the anger burning inside him. The forest fell silent when he approached, the animals sensing the predator nearby. The birds, the scurrying animals, the chatter of insects all seemed to vanish whenever he passed, leaving only the weight of his presence.

The forest had always held this silence for him, but today it felt darker, a fitting stillness for the rage that had taken root within him.

His sister had been so young, barely more than a pup. He

had led her along that trail, intending to show her the forest he knew so well. He, her older brother, her protector. But he had failed, clouded by overconfidence, and her life had slipped through his claws while he struggled with the cold, unyielding metal of the humans' trap. The steel jaws had refused to give way, and he'd been forced to watch helplessly as her breaths grew shallow, then ceased altogether.

The rules he'd followed for years—the unspoken border between his pack and the humans—seemed meaningless now. His kind had learned long ago to stay away from the humans, to observe silently, unseen and undisturbed. As a young pup, he had watched them from a distance, curious about the way they moved in the world, surrounded by strange contraptions and weapons. He had seen their fire, their loud gatherings, the way they ventured into the forest only briefly, and he had known to stay hidden.

And though he'd stayed close to observe them over the years, he had kept the distance that all in his pack had learned to keep. Humans were dangerous, their boom sticks deadly. They did not think like the pack, did not understand the rhythm of the forest. And so they had always existed on the edge of his world, something to avoid, to keep at bay.

But now, the rules were gone, burned away by the memory of her eyes—wide with pain, her body contorted in agony as the steel trap clamped around her leg. She had never seen it coming, and he had been too late to save her.

The scent of the humans had clung to that metal, sharp and cold, a reminder of who had taken her life. And when they had come back, he had taken out his fury on them, his claws cutting through their flesh, his fangs biting deep. But the rage had not subsided; it only grew, fed by the injustice of her death, by the humans' arrogance in thinking they could enter his world without consequences.

He rose from the creek, his heavy muscles rippling beneath his fur as he gazed toward the mountains. Over those jagged peaks, across the valleys and ridges of dense forest, lay the human settlement, distant yet close enough to sense their presence. They had their walls, their lights, their boom sticks, believing these defenses made them safe. But he had watched them long enough to know better.

For all their noise and confidence, he understood that they were fragile creatures, vulnerable in ways they didn't realize. And they would soon learn the cost of crossing into his world, of taking something that could never be replaced.

He thought of his pack, the life he could never return to. The guilt weighed too heavily; he was no longer the creature who had once run with them.

The silence of the forest deepened around him as he moved, his rage casting a darkness over the peaceful morning. This was a new path, one without the rules that had kept him safe. He no longer cared for safety. He no longer cared for the boundary they had once respected.

All he wanted was revenge.

TWO

Deputy Delvaney sat behind the front desk at the sheriff's office, idly flipping through reports and sipping coffee. It was a typical Monday, slow and uneventful, until the front door swung open with a creak.

A disheveled woman strode in, her steps quick, her face hardened by years of tough living. She wasn't striking in the traditional sense—her sharp features and weathered skin told a different story. She'd lived rough, likely done more than her fair share of drugs, and it showed in the hollow look in her eyes and the slight jitter in her hands.

Delvaney glanced up from his paperwork, recognizing her immediately. Angel, Tucker Leney's girl. And where there was talk of Tucker, there was usually trouble.

"I need to file a missing person report," Angel said, skipping any formalities as she marched up to the counter.

Delvaney raised an eyebrow, setting his coffee down. "Who's missing?"

"Tucker," she said, crossing her arms defensively. "I haven't seen him for three days now and we've got bills to pay. He left real early Friday morning, said he was going to meet up with Bo Reyes, and he never came back."

Delvaney let out a small sigh, pulling out the necessary paperwork. Tucker Leney and Bo Reyes. The town's resident troublemakers. Always looking for a quick, often illegal, buck. Everyone in the sheriff's department knew those names too well.

"And you're just now filing a report?" Delvaney asked, grabbing his pen.

Angel shifted, looking slightly annoyed. "I thought he'd show up. He's done this before, but three days is too long. He's never gone this long without at least texting me."

Delvaney nodded slowly, jotting down the basic details. "So, he was with Bo Reyes?"

"Yeah," Angel replied, her voice sharp. "They were gonna do some work or whatever. I didn't ask too many questions. That's not my business."

Of course, it wasn't. Tucker and Bo's line of work was always shady.

Delvaney kept writing but paused, glancing up. "Would you like to file a report on Bo as well?"

Angel rolled her eyes. "I don't care about Bo."

Delvaney's eyebrow lifted slightly. "Have you tried calling him? Maybe he knows where Tucker is."

Angel scoffed, her irritation flaring. "Of course I tried calling him. I'm not an idiot! His phone went straight to his stupid voicemail."

Delvaney jotted it down, though it didn't come as much of a surprise. Bo and Tucker had a way of disappearing off the radar. He sighed, pulling more details from Angel, but knew that without knowing where they'd gone, finding them would be nearly impossible.

"So, you have no idea where they might've gone? Did Tucker say anything before he left?"

"No," she replied with a shrug. "He didn't say, and I didn't ask."

Typical, Delvaney thought. Tucker and Bo were secretive about their ventures, usually because they didn't want anyone knowing what they were up to.

Delvaney wrote the information down, though it wasn't much to go on. "Any chance they left town?"

"If they did, he didn't tell me—he knows I'd kill him if he had," Angel replied, her tone sharp with irritation.

The deputy lifted an eyebrow. "Probably not the place to say that kind of thing, ma'am," Delvaney said.

He paused, studying her before jotting down a few more notes. Delvaney had dealt with Tucker and Bo more times than he cared to admit, and he knew this wasn't going to be an easy case. Those two could've gone anywhere, doing anything—and more than likely, it wasn't legal.

"So, what now?" Angel asked, her arms still crossed, the impatience clear in her voice. "Are you going to go look for him or what?"

"We'll keep an eye out," Delvaney said, keeping his tone calm. "But without knowing where they went, it's hard to start a search. Tucker's an adult, and if he didn't tell you where he was going, he probably didn't want anyone to know."

Angel let out an irritated huff. "And what am I supposed to do if he doesn't show up? How am I supposed to pay rent at the end of the week?"

Delvaney blinked, surprised by her focus on rent rather than Tucker's well-being. "I'm sure Tucker will turn up soon," he said softly. "And when he does, you can figure things out."

"Yeah, right," she muttered, turning on her heel and heading for the door. "Freakin' useless."

Delvaney watched her go, the door slamming behind her as she left. Tucker and Bo were trouble, no doubt about it, but three days was a long time for even them to be missing.

Filing the report, Delvaney couldn't shake the nagging feeling that something was off this time. Tucker and Bo had disappeared before, but this felt different. Where had they gone? And what had they gotten into?

THREE

"I told you we should've turned back hours ago," Lindsey said, her voice edged with frustration as she walked a few paces ahead of Tom, not bothering to hide her irritation.

Tom sighed, shifting the weight of his backpack. "Yeah, yeah, I heard you the first twenty times. But look, we've got a good spot here. Let's just set up and relax for a bit."

Lindsey shot him a look but didn't argue. She was too tired to keep up the fight, and the idea of setting up camp was enough to finally put their bickering on pause.

They'd been hiking since early afternoon, and the excitement that started the day had soured into exhaustion.

The rough terrain, aching feet, and constant snags along the trail had worn down their patience. When they finally found a small trailhead campsite surrounded by towering pines, relief swept over them. The sky overhead was fading to a dusky purple, hinting that nightfall wasn't far off, and the air around them held the quiet chill of evening.

As they set down their packs and took a moment to catch their breath, Lindsey glanced around, almost smiling despite herself. Hiking and exploring had always been their thing—a love they both shared. Salt Lake City could feel stifling, and getting lost in the wilderness, even on rough days like this one, was their way of reconnecting.

Lindsey remarked, "This is fine, but you're the one making dinner."

Tom smirked, though he was too tired to keep up the banter. "I'll get right on it, your majesty."

They worked in silence for the next hour, the tension between them slowly dissipating as they set up the tent, gathered firewood, and got a small fire going. By the time the fire was crackling warmly and the smell of grilled frankfurts filled the air, their earlier argument felt distant.

"I'll admit," Lindsey said, sitting down on a log near the

fire, "this is nice."

Tom grinned, handing her a plate. "Told you we'd find a good spot. We just needed to push through."

Lindsey rolled her eyes but smiled. "I'm not giving you full credit, but yeah… this isn't so bad."

As they ate, the forest around them came alive with the usual night sounds. Crickets chirped, the occasional hoot of an owl echoed through the trees, and the fire crackled softly, its light casting flickering shades across their faces.

Tom threw another log onto the fire and leaned back, finally letting his body relax. "Alright, truce?" he said, holding up his drink.

Lindsey clinked her bottle against his, smiling. "Truce."

As the fire crackled and the tension from earlier faded, Lindsey leaned back with a sigh, gazing into the flames. She glanced at Tom, her expression softening. "Hey… I'm sorry for my mood today," she said quietly. "I've been really stressed out because of work and my mom's illness."

Tom smiled, reaching out to squeeze her hand. "I get it, babe. I'm glad we're here. Away from all that, just the two of us." He raised his bottle in a playful toast. "To taking a break from reality, even if it's just for a couple of days."

She laughed, clinking her bottle against his. "Cheers to that."

The fire's warmth and the shared moment melted the last remnants of the day's tension. Smiling, Lindsey stood up to stretch. "I'm going to grab another drink from the cooler. Want one?"

"Sure," Tom replied, grinning as she walked off, feeling the peace of the wilderness settle over them.

Tom looked on while she headed towards the cooler they had hidden close to their campsite. The firelight flickered across her figure as she stepped just beyond its warmth, her form now mostly a silhouette. He stretched his arms above his head and leaned back, staring up at the stars starting to appear in the clear night sky.

That's when he heard it.

A sharp snap—like a twig breaking—came from the darkness behind their camp. In an instant, his body tightened and his senses sharpened.

"Wait, Lindsey," Tom called out, jumping up and swiftly turning towards the source of the noise. His eyes searched the dark tree line that surrounded their camp. "Did you hear that?"

Lindsey paused, her hand already on the cooler. She glanced back at him, raising an eyebrow. "Hear what?"

"There was something—" Tom's voice dropped, his head tilted as he listened, eyes narrowing toward the darkened line of trees beyond their campsite. Just as he strained to hear, another sharp crack rang out, this time closer, and a prickle of dread washed over him. "Did you hear that?"

Lindsey rolled her eyes, turning back to the cooler. "It's probably just a deer. Or a raccoon. Relax."

Tom didn't move, his heart thudding harder as he scanned the woods, every instinct on high alert. "Lindsey, we're in grizzly country. Could be more than a raccoon." His gaze didn't leave the trees as he spoke, his senses telling him that something was off.

The forest, which had felt peaceful and safe moments before, now seemed... wrong. It was too quiet, as though every creature around them had suddenly gone still.

Then they both heard it.

A deep, rumbling growl. The sound was low, guttural, and

too damn close.

Lindsey froze, her hand hovering above the cooler. Her heart pounded in her chest as she slowly turned to face Tom, her wide eyes locking with his.

Tom swallowed, his throat suddenly dry. "That... doesn't sound like a raccoon or a deer."

The growl came again, this time deeper, vibrating through the ground beneath their feet. Tom had never experienced a sound like this before; it was primal and dangerous, triggering every instinct in his body to flee.

"Lindsey," Tom whispered, his voice trembling. "Get back here. Now."

Hesitation overcame Lindsey as fear gripped her muscles and anxiety crept in. She wanted to move, to run, but her legs refused to cooperate. Slowly, she took a step back toward the fire, her eyes darting around the campsite.

"Please tell me it's not a bear," she pleaded, her voice quivering, barely audible.

Tom didn't answer right away, his gaze fixed on the dark line of trees beyond the firelight. The crackling flames suddenly felt too small, too feeble against the vast, encroaching darkness. A flicker of unease crept in as he thought of the can of bear spray still clipped to his backpack, just out of reach.

Then, from the brush at the rim of the firelight, it emerged.

A hulking, monstrous figure on all fours stepped out from the trees, its yellow eyes glowing with an unnatural intensity. The creature was massive, its broad, muscular frame tense as it moved with terrifying quiet, like a shadow brought to life. Its powerful limbs and elongated, clawed hands flexed as it stalked forward, each step radiating controlled, predatory intent. It stopped just short of the firelight, hovering in the dark, its eyes fixed on them with a hunger that seemed almost... aware.

Lindsey's breath caught in her throat, her mind struggling to comprehend the hideous thing standing before them. This wasn't an animal. This wasn't something she had ever thought could exist.

As it stepped into the firelight, they both gasped in fright and disbelief. Its face resembled a twisted, nightmarish wolf, features locked in a permanent snarl. Lips curled back, exposing rows of bloodstained teeth, while thick saliva dripped from its long, razor-sharp fangs.

Tom was the first to break the silence. "Run!" he shouted, his voice hoarse with terror.

But it was too late.

In an instant, the creature lunged at him, moving with a speed and ferocity that was impossible for something so large. Tom barely had time to raise his arms before the creature was on him, knocking him to the ground with a force that sent the breath from his lungs.

Lindsey screamed, stumbling backward as the beast tore into Tom, its claws slashing through his clothes and into his flesh. Blood sprayed into the air as Tom's screams echoed through the forest, his body writhing beneath the relentless assault.

"Tom!" Lindsey cried, her voice shrill with fear. But she couldn't move, couldn't do anything but watch in horror as the creature ripped into him, tearing at his chest, his arms, his face.

Lindsey's instincts finally kicked in, and she turned and ran, her heart pounding as she stumbled through the dark. She hadn't gone far when she spotted a tree and crouched low behind it, her breath coming in fast and shallow. Tom's desperate, gurgling screams echoed through the forest, the creature's growls mixing with the sickening sound of tearing flesh. Paralyzed with fear, her body trembled, but she didn't dare move. She was only a few steps away from the horror behind her, and she knew she couldn't stay there.

Ahead, she spotted a tall pine tree with low branches—her only hope. Without thinking, she leaped at the tree, grabbing onto the lowest branch and scrambling up, her nails digging into the rough bark as she hauled herself higher and higher. With adrenaline and fear coursing through her, her arms trembled with the effort.

Once she reached a high enough point, out of the creature's grasp, she paused and rested against the tree. She gasped frantically, her chest rising and falling rapidly. She looked down, her eyes scanning the ground below.

Through the flickering light, she could just make out the fire still burning at their campsite. The creature was there, crouched over Tom's body, its massive form blocking most of what was happening. But she didn't need to see. She knew.

It was eating him.

Tears streamed down her face as she tried to quiet her sobs. Her body shook with fear, but she couldn't afford to make a sound. She clamped her hand over her mouth, trying to stifle the sobs that threatened to escape.

From her perch in the tree, she watched in horror as the creature tore into Tom's body. The sickening sounds of bones snapping and flesh tearing filled the air. Her stomach churned, and she fought back the urge to vomit. Squeezing her eyes shut, she whispered, *"Please, God, make it stop."*

Hours passed.

The night was long and agonizing. Lindsey remained frozen in the tree, too terrified to move, her legs aching from staying crouched in the same position for so long. She was too horrified to do anything but listen. Below her, the sounds of the beast's gruesome feast echoed through the darkness— wet, tearing noises, bones snapping, and the occasional growl that sent chills down her spine. She couldn't stop trembling, her tears mixing with the cold sweat on her skin. She pressed her back against the rough bark, trying to make herself as small as possible, clinging to the tree as if it were her lifeline.

Lindsey kept her eyes shut, willing herself not to look, not to think about the horror playing out below. But the image of Tom—her Tom, reduced to nothing more than a pile of broken flesh—flashed relentlessly in her mind. She wanted to scream, wanted to release the grief and horror building inside her, but the need to survive was stronger. She couldn't give herself away. She couldn't let the creature know she was still there.

The fire had now died down to embers, casting only faint, flickering light over the camp. In the near-total darkness, her other senses sharpened. Every crackle from the fire, every rustle of leaves made her flinch.

She had to stay quiet. She had to stay hidden.

Suddenly, she sat up, realizing the sound of the creature devouring had stopped. The wet, tearing noises had vanished, leaving only an eerie silence. Her heart raced as panic seized her; she hadn't heard it leave. The only thing more terrifying than its growls was the silence that followed. Every muscle in her body tensed, locked in place, as she resisted the urge to move or breathe. What if it was still down there, lurking and waiting for her to make a fatal mistake?

Hours passed, or at least it felt like it. The forest had long since gone quiet. There were no more growls, no more sounds of feeding. But Lindsey remained perched in the tree, her legs cramping painfully, her breath shallow and measured, afraid that even the slightest movement could attract the creature's attention.

The night seemed endless, stretching on with unbearable tension. Eventually, as the first light of dawn began to touch the horizon, the forest stirred. Birds started to chirp tentatively, as though testing whether it was safe to break the silence. The early morning breeze rustled through the branches, and for the first time in hours, Lindsey dared to open her eyes.

The clearing below was still. She blinked through her tears, her vision adjusting to the pale light creeping over the landscape. What had once been their camp—where she and Tom had laughed, argued, and shared dinner—was now a scene of devastation. The fire was little more than a pile of smoldering ash, and their belongings were scattered and destroyed.

And Tom...

She forced herself to look at the spot where the creature had attacked him. What remained of his body was barely recognizable. Torn clothes, splintered bones, and shredded flesh lay in a pool of dried blood. The sight was more than she could bear. With bile rising in her throat, she averted her head quickly, her stomach lurching, but she controlled it.

It's gone. The thought finally registered. The beast was gone.

With every inch of her body aching and numb from

sitting crouched for so long, Lindsey shifted slightly, trying to get some feeling back in her legs before she climbed down. Slowly, she forced herself to move, her legs shaky and weak as she descended.

As Lindsey climbed down, she kept whispering to herself, *Move. You have to move. Find help.* Each time her foot touched a new branch, she froze, gripping the bark, her eyes darting over the darkness below. She stopped several times, holding her breath, glancing around to see if the creature was still out there, waiting for her to come down.

But the forest was quiet.

Come on. Just a little more. She forced herself to keep going, her limbs trembling as she neared the ground, nerves stretched to the breaking point. Finally, her feet touched the forest floor, but she lingered, looking around, making sure it was safe before she took a tentative step away from the tree.

But nothing happened.

Before Lindsey could reach the road, she realized the only way out was past Tom's remains. She took a shuddering breath, forcing herself to step around the scattered pieces, each step pulling her closer to the road but forcing her past the horror she'd just survived. Her body trembled as she willed herself not to look down, the urge to cry pressing hard against her chest, but she held it back. There was no time for that now. She had to keep going.

Her shoes crunched over rocks and branches as she moved forward, barely registering the forest around her. Her only focus was escape. She kept pausing, glancing over her shoulder, her heart racing with the fear that the creature was creeping up behind her.

When she finally broke through the trees onto the dirt road, a wave of relief washed over her, momentarily numbing her exhaustion. She stumbled forward, her vision blurring as she pushed herself onward, knowing she couldn't stop. Not yet.

Just as she rounded a bend in the road, she saw it—a faint glimmer in the distance. A car. She could hardly believe her eyes, her breath catching as she forced herself into a weak sprint, waving her arms desperately.

"Help!" she managed to shout, her voice cracked from fear and exhaustion. "Please... help!"

The car slowed, sending up a small cloud of dust as the driver pulled over. A man stepped out, his face a mix of confusion and concern as he took in her terror-stricken appearance.

"Hey! Are you okay? What happened?" His voice was calm but urgent, his eyes darting to the trees around them as if sensing the fear radiating from her.

Lindsey collapsed to her knees in front of him, clutching at his jacket, her hands trembling. "It killed Tom... there's something in the woods," she whispered, her voice barely audible. "It... was a monster..."

The man's face turned pale, but he gently helped her to her feet and guided her into the passenger seat, his gaze sweeping the woods before he buckled her in and started the engine.

The shocked stranger whipped the car into a tight U-turn before hurrying down the winding road toward safety. Lindsey stared blankly out the window, her mind looping through every horrifying detail: the creature, Tom's final scream, those piercing yellow eyes—each memory etched into her mind like a scar. Even as the dense forest gave way to the familiar signs of civilization, she knew she'd never truly escape what she'd witnessed.

She had survived, but the memory of the monster lurking in those woods would haunt her forever.

FOUR

The dogman crouched low, its massive form concealed within the dense underbrush. It could still taste the blood on its tongue, the remnants of its feast clinging to its fanged jaws. The male had been more than enough to satisfy its hunger for the night, and the woman who had scrambled up the tree had posed no threat. She was frozen with terror, and the scent of her fear lingered in the air, sharper than the coppery tang of blood. Normally, it could have leapt up and torn her down in seconds, but the thrill of the chase had faded; it had already made its kill.

It had no need to worry about the humans. The woman had fled the camp, likely still cowering in that tree. It didn't care about her anymore. Not now. There were plenty more humans in these woods. Their scent was everywhere, and soon, as the sun fell again, it would hunt.

But first, it needed to recover.

As the sun climbed higher, the dogman shifted its position, seeking a deeper part of the forest where it could hide from the encroaching daylight. The sun didn't burn it, but it didn't relish being exposed in the open, either. Its keen senses had adapted to hunting in the dark, stalking through the night where it could remain unseen, unheard, until it was too late for its prey to escape.

It lumbered deeper into the woods, the underbrush growing thicker as it moved. There was a small, secluded hollow in the earth that it had used before, a place far enough from any human trail that it could sleep without being disturbed.

When it reached the hollow, the creature collapsed onto the damp earth, its massive frame weary. It lay still, breath slowing as it sank into the cool soil.

Soon, it would feast again.

FIVE

Sheriff Ronald Becan stood at the edge of what had once been a peaceful campsite, now transformed into a scene of raw carnage. The campfire was reduced to cold ash, its warmth long gone. Beyond it, the ground was stained with blood—far more blood than Becan had ever wanted to see in one place.

Tom's remains had already been covered with a tarp, but the outline of what was left was disturbing enough. Scattered gear lay abandoned, ripped open, and discarded. The whole place reeked of death.

Sheriff Becan narrowed his eyes, his hands shoved deep into the pockets of his jacket. He stood with his weight shifted onto one foot, his belly pressing against the worn leather of his belt. He'd been sheriff in these parts for over a decade, and in that time, he'd dealt with more than his share of drunk drivers, domestic disputes, and missing livestock. But this? This was new. And the sight of it was more than he wanted to handle on a quiet morning.

The sheriff sucked on the end of a cigarette and let the smoke hang lazily in his lungs before exhaling slowly. The cigarette was half-heartedly flicked away into the dirt. Becan scratched at his stubbled chin, his beady eyes darting from the destroyed campsite to his Chief Deputy, John Perry, who was kneeling a few feet away, inspecting the ground around the victim.

"Jesus," Perry muttered under his breath as he rose to his feet. "It's worse than I expected."

"Yup," Becan grunted, his voice heavy with indifference. "But people die all the time out here. Wolves, bears, hell— people do dumb shit and get lost. Not our first rodeo, Perry."

But Perry sensed this was different.

John Perry had been Becan's Chief Deputy for nearly five years, and while he was younger than the sheriff by a good twenty years, he had more integrity in his little finger than

Becan had in his whole bloated frame. Perry stood tall, his lean, wiry build honed from years of hiking these woods on his own time. He believed in the duty of law enforcement—to serve and protect—and it chafed at him to see how Becan ran things.

Perry's lips pressed into a hard line as he stood, the morning sun glinting off the badge pinned to his chest. He was a Wyoming boy through and through, born and raised in the mountains, with a deep respect for the land and the people. His father had been a rancher, his mother a schoolteacher, and he'd learned early on the values of hard work, decency, and standing up for what was right.

But Becan? Becan was another story.

The sheriff had rolled into the town of Enrick more than a decade ago, setting himself up in a position of power that, Perry suspected, he hadn't earned. There were rumors about how Becan had gotten the sheriff's job, whispers that he was connected to some of the seedier elements of the county—backroom deals, money changing hands, favors traded in secret. It also helped that his brother-in-law was the town's Mayor. He'd never been caught in anything concrete, but the town's folk didn't like or trust him. They called him lazy, untrustworthy, and just smart enough to keep his neck out of a noose.

Perry, on the other hand, had built up a reputation of his own. He wasn't flashy, wasn't the type to stand out in a crowd, but he was good at what he did. People respected him, and in private, many of them wondered why Perry hadn't tried to take the sheriff's job for himself. He was competent, hard-working, and he actually cared about the town and its people. But for now, he remained the Chief Deputy, stuck doing the hard work while Becan took credit for it.

Perry cleaned his hands with antiseptic wipes, his face tense as he turned back to the sheriff. "Sheriff, this wasn't a bear or a wolf," he said, his voice low. "I'm no biologist, but those bite marks are way too large for either of them."

Becan rolled his eyes, pulling a can of chewing tobacco from his pocket and tapping it lightly against his palm before stuffing a wad into his cheek.

"Perry, relax. The girl probably freaked out and got her animals mixed up. City folk. They come out here thinking every sound in the woods is a monster ready to eat 'em."

He spat a stream of tobacco juice onto the ground, just inches from the blood-soaked dirt. "We'll write it up, clear the scene, and let the coroner do his job. Case closed."

But Perry couldn't just let it go. He knelt again, his fingers tracing the drag marks in the dirt. Tom's body had been ripped apart, violently so. Whatever had attacked him had done so with brutal, unchecked force. The poor bastard hadn't stood a chance. Lindsey, the girl who had barely escaped, was still in shock. She hadn't been able to say much, but one thing had come through clearly:

It was a monster.

Perry couldn't forget the fear in her eyes when she'd said it. "It was huge," she had whispered, her voice trembling. "Like a wolf mixed with a hyena… but much bigger. It had piercing yellow eyes… too many teeth and its fur was covered in blood."

That detail troubled him as he studied the ground. Deep footprints pressed into the dirt, each one edged with long, sharp indents—claw marks. Something heavy had moved through here, leaving a trail from the forest edge to the center of camp. Perry followed the tracks to where the trees thickened, each clawed print marking a steady approach. The ground around them was uneven, churned where the creature's powerful claws had dug in with every step, as though it had been moving with purpose.

"What're you doing, Perry?" Becan's voice cut through his thoughts, sounding lazy and disinterested. He hadn't moved from his spot, arms crossed over his chest, his gut pushing his gun belt up as he spat another stream of tobacco.

Perry straightened and walked over to his backpack. "I need to photograph the scene."

Becan chuckled, his lips curling into a condescending smile. "A big ol' wolf, huh? Sure, and maybe it was a bear, or maybe she saw a coyote. These city folks can barely tell a deer from a rabbit." He scanned the scene with exaggerated indifference. "So, she saw a big animal. It's tragic, sure, but we're not wasting time chasing some wild creature."

Perry clenched his jaw, trying to hold back his frustration. "Sheriff, you didn't see her. She wasn't just scared—she was terrified. She saw something, and it shook her to her core."

Becan shrugged, giving an unimpressed wave. "Yeah, well, people get spooked out here all the time. As far as I'm concerned, this is just another wildlife run-in." He gestured toward the coroner and his team, who were walking up the trail. "We'll get the remains back to the morgue, file a report, and move on. Not worth stirring up a panic over some 'monster' story from a girl who's had a scare."

Becan spat on the bloodstained ground, wiping his mouth with the back of his hand. "Make sure the coroner does his job right, Perry," he added, turning away. "Oh, and Fish and Game are on their way too." He gave a quick, dismissive nod before heading back to his car. "I'll be at the office."

As Becan sauntered back to his truck, leaving Perry standing by the campsite, the frustration inside Perry boiled over. He had grown used to Becan's dismissive attitude over the years, but this time it felt different. More serious. Whatever had killed Tom wasn't just an animal—it was something dangerous, something that didn't belong in these woods. He had no doubt about that.

Perry knew the sheriff wasn't going to do a damn thing about it. He'd sign off on the coroner's report, brush it off as a freak accident, and move on. But Perry wasn't wired that way. He couldn't ignore the facts just because they were inconvenient, and he sure as hell wasn't about to let this go without doing a little more digging.

He crouched by the edge of the clearing again, his keen eyes scanning the ground where the tracks led into the woods. The footprints. The blood. The sheer violence of the attack. This wasn't a simple case of a bear getting too close to a campsite or a wolf attacking out of desperation. It was deliberate. Calculated.

Perry's gut told him that whatever had attacked Tom, it wasn't a bear or a wolf. It was something worse. Something he had never encountered before.

He sighed, running a hand through his short, brown hair. He could feel the weight of the responsibility resting on his shoulders. The town didn't know what had happened out here yet, and Becan would do everything he could to keep it that way. But if Perry was right—and he felt in his bones that he was—then the town of Enrick had a serious problem on its hands.

He rose to his feet, scanning the woods one last time. The wind rustled through the trees, and for a moment, he thought he heard something. A faint growl, carried on the breeze.

Perry's hand instinctively went to the gun at his side, his heart racing. But the noise faded, and the woods returned to silence.

Whatever was out there, he thought, it's not done.

As he made his way back to the crime scene, he resolved to dig deeper into this case. If Becan wasn't going to do his job, then Perry would.

Because something out here was hunting—and it wouldn't stop with just one.

SIX

Chief Deputy Perry's truck rumbled along the Wyoming highway, flanked by towering pines that loomed in the cool evening air. The sun had long dipped below the horizon, painting the sky in fading hues of deep purple and orange as night fell over the vast landscape. As he drove, the road stretched out in front of him like a dark ribbon, winding through familiar terrain that had become more than just scenery over the years—it was home.

His thoughts drifted to the campsite incident, the grisly details of the scene sticking with him in a way he didn't often experience. He'd seen plenty working for the department: bar fights that went too far, thefts, accidents, but the scene at Tom's campsite unsettled him. The coroner's initial assessment suggested a wolf attack, but something about it seemed off, different from the patterns Perry had encountered before. And Lindsey's face—the horror he saw in her eyes as she recounted the attack—lingered in his mind. Wolves and even bears were hardly out of place in Wyoming, but this was unlike anything he'd dealt with.

As he turned onto the narrow dirt road toward his home, the headlights cut through the darkened trees, illuminating patches of dense underbrush on either side. Just as he rounded a bend, a movement in the shadows caught his eye, a brief flash as something shifted between the trees. He shook his head, forcing himself to dismiss it as a trick of the light. The woods were alive at night, and he knew better than anyone how shadows could play with the mind.

Pulling into his gravel driveway, Perry let the familiar quiet of the woods settle around him. His house, a small, unassuming one-story, sat isolated on the edge of town—a peaceful spot he'd chosen deliberately. The stillness usually helped him unwind, a sanctuary from the demands of his role.

Inside, Perry kicked off his boots and made his way to the bathroom for a quick shower. Hot water hit his shoulders, easing the tension that had gathered throughout the day, and he closed his eyes, letting the steam envelop him. Lately, he'd found himself spending more time than usual lost in thought.

His career had brought stability, structure, but there were nights when he wondered if it had been too consuming. He'd once pictured a different life for himself, one filled with family and a partner to come home to. But that life had faded into the background years ago, replaced by the steady hum of routine and the familiar faces of Enrick's townsfolk.

After his shower, Perry dressed in jeans and a worn button-up, pulling a jacket over his shoulders before heading out the door. His brother, Jack, had insisted on meeting for dinner, and Perry knew Jack well enough to know that a "quick meal" meant a couple of hours of catching up over burgers and beers. Jack was his older brother by five years, a family man with a knack for keeping Perry grounded.

Stone's Grill sat on the edge of town, a staple for locals and travelers alike. The neon sign glowed warm against the night, casting a beacon of light across the parking lot. Perry found Jack waiting at a booth near the back, nursing a beer and scrolling through his phone. The moment he spotted Perry, he stood up with a grin.

"About time, little brother," Jack teased, giving him a quick hug as he motioned for Perry to sit. "Thought you'd skip out on me again."

Perry rolled his eyes, sliding into the booth. "Not my fault you pick the busiest days to plan dinner."

They ordered drinks, and Jack wasted no time diving into conversation, recounting stories about his family. Jack had a wife and four kids, a life Perry had always thought he'd have, but watching his brother talk about his hectic home with such affection made Perry feel a mix of admiration and gratitude—he might not have that life, but he was glad his brother did.

Jack's stories shifted to Scarlet's horseback riding and little Charlie's habit of climbing everything in sight, the joy in his voice making Perry smile. He might have his doubts about his own choices, but listening to Jack was a reminder that there were different kinds of fulfillment.

After the waitress brought their food, Jack glanced at him thoughtfully. "I heard about the attack at the campground," he said, keeping his tone casual, though his eyes were probing. "What happened?"

Perry put down his drink, choosing his words carefully. "We had a camper attacked out there. His girlfriend managed to get away, but... it wasn't pretty. Coroner thinks it was a wolf, but I'm not sure."

Jack watched him, taking in the words. "Damn. Must have

been a hell of a sight."

"Yeah. I can't shake the feeling something's off about it, though. We'll know more once the coroner has the report done."

Jack took a sip of his drink, nodding as he processed the information. "Well, you always follow your gut. If something's wrong, you'll figure it out."

They finished their meal, exchanging stories from the week and the usual ribbing that brothers traded. When they stepped out into the crisp night air, Jack clapped him on the shoulder.

"Promise you'll make it over for dinner soon," Jack said. "Scarlet won't stop asking when you're taking her fishing."

Perry chuckled. "I'll bring her out soon—maybe Saturday."

Jack grinned. "Good. Maybe she'll teach you a thing or two about catching fish."

They laughed, and Perry climbed into his truck, watching Jack wave as he drove off. The roads were quiet as he made his way home, his headlights sweeping over the familiar trees and brush. His thoughts drifted back to the attack, questions still circling in his mind, but the memory of Jack's stories lingered, a reminder of the life he had chosen and the one he hadn't. Whatever this case turned out to be, he'd see it through.

SEVEN

Twilight had long since passed when the dogman stirred, rising from its hiding place as darkness settled over the Wyoming landscape. Sheltered in the dense undergrowth, it had waited for the cover of night to cloak its movements. As the forest hushed and darkness crept in, it became poised for hunting.

Hunger clawed at its insides, sharper than before, spurring it onward. It had rested through the day, sheltered from the light, its senses sharp and primed. But the primal need to feed outweighed all else, forcing it to slip into the night once more.

Moving with a predatory silence, it stalked through the

trees, muscles rippling beneath its thick coat as it maneuvered with practiced stealth. The creature knew this land well—the slopes, the trails, and the creeks that wound through the wilderness and down toward the human settlement. Instinct told it to stay hidden, but hunger drove it on, overriding its wariness.

A faint scent hung in the air, drifting from a nearby river and mingling with the damp, earthy smell of the forest. The dogman tilted its head, nostrils flaring, eyes narrowing as it pinpointed the direction of its next prey. Nearby insects buzzed into silence, their instincts kicking in, warning them of the deadly presence moving among them. The owls grew quiet, their keen senses recognizing the silent threat, and soon, the entire forest stilled in reverent fear.

The dogman pressed on, feeding off the silence. The hunt had begun.

Tonight, it crept closer to the edge of the human settlement. Not into the dense clusters of houses where humans gathered in numbers, but to the isolated outskirts where they lived far from each other, separated by open stretches of land and thick clusters of trees. Here, where they relied on their isolation for security, the dogman knew it could find easy prey.

It emerged from the forest's edge, its yellow eyes glowing faintly as it scanned the landscape before it. Scattered lights dotted the hillsides—farmhouses set apart, each with enough land and woods to give it cover. These humans believed they were safe in the quiet, unlit spaces between them. But they were wrong.

The dogman slunk forward, keeping low to the ground, using the tall grass and rugged terrain to conceal its massive form. It approached the closest house, a wide, sprawling farmhouse with a single light over the front porch that flickered in the night. From here, it could smell the human inside, the scent drawing it closer, filling it with a growing need to feed.

It paused just beyond the porch light's reach, crouching in the darkness as it listened for signs of movement. Inside, it heard footsteps—one human moving about in the stillness. Alone. The dogman's mouth watered, its claws flexing into the earth. But it waited, watching the house with an intensity that spoke to its patience.

From the dark, it observed the human's slow, predictable movements through the window. The quiet clink of dishes. The creak of floorboards. And finally, the door opening. The man stepped out onto the porch, stretching, unaware of the predator lurking just beyond the light. He rubbed his eyes, checking his phone, entirely oblivious.

The dogman's body tensed, its muscles coiling in preparation to lunge, to taste flesh, to feed. But then, as if by instinct, the man turned and retreated back into the house, the door clicking shut behind him.

The dogman crouched, frustration twisting through it as it stared at the empty porch. Unwilling to wait longer to satisfy its hunger, it slunk back into the cover of darkness, scanning the fields for another target. The night was still young, and more humans lay scattered across the outskirts—vulnerable, isolated, and unaware of the danger that crept among them.

Moving swiftly along the forest's edge, the dogman caught the faint scent of two females drifting on the breeze. It came from a house bordered on three sides by thick woods. Perfect.

With silent, measured steps, the creature slipped forward, hunger sharpening its senses.

EIGHT

The smell of freshly baked lasagna filled the cozy kitchen, where Sofia and Layla sat at the table, forks in hand, sharing a quiet dinner. The overhead light cast a soft glow over the room, making the house feel warm and inviting, a sanctuary against the cold darkness that had already settled outside.

"This is so good, Layla. You're spoiling me," Sofia said, her voice teasing as she took another bite of lasagna.

Layla smiled, rolling her eyes. "If I didn't cook, you'd be living on takeout and energy drinks."

Sofia shrugged with a grin. "Probably. But that's why I've got you, right?"

Layla laughed, shaking her head. "Felix's getting the same treatment later. I left the rest in the oven for him. He said he will be starving after his shift."

Sofia raised an eyebrow. "How late is he working tonight?"

"He should be here soon," Layla replied. "Just needs to finish up with a few animals at the clinic."

Sofia leaned back in her chair, her eyes drifting toward the dark windows. The night outside was pitch black, with only the porch light illuminating the yard. It always got this dark out on the outskirts, far away from the town's streetlights. It used to make her uneasy, the thick darkness that pressed in on the house at night, but she'd gotten used to it over the years.

"Glad it's a quiet night. I've got Vince's bike to work on in the shed," Sofia said after a moment, looking down at her plate. "Promised him I'd have it tuned up by the weekend. He's been bugging me about it all week."

"Of course," Layla replied with a smirk, taking a sip of water. "You spend more time out there with those bikes than you do in the house."

Sofia grinned, leaning in with a playful glint in her eye. "I just like staying busy. Besides, you get the whole place to yourself and your loooover when I'm out there. It's a win-win."

Layla shook her head, smiling. "True. But I wouldn't mind if you joined me on the couch every once in a while for a movie night. You know, like normal sisters."

Sofia chuckled, reaching for her water. "Normal sisters don't have to fix everyone's motorcycles after dinner. But I'll think about it. Maybe next time."

"Uh-huh, I'll believe it when I see it."

After dinner, Sofia helped clear the table while Layla stored the lasagna leftovers in the oven to keep warm for Felix, who was due any minute now. The kitchen was clean and organized in no time, the way Layla liked it.

"Thanks for dinner, L," Sofia said, slinging her jacket over her shoulder as she made her way to the door. "I'll be in the shed if you need me. Shouldn't be too long tonight."

Layla glanced out the window toward the shed that sat a few dozen yards away from the house, its light already glowing faintly through the darkness. "You've got the lights on out there, right?"

"I will. It'll be bright as day in there," Sofia said with a grin.

"Don't worry. I'll be fine."

"Alright, but be careful. It's creepy out there when it gets this dark."

Sofia smirked. "You sound like Mom. I'll be fine, L. Go relax. I'll see you in a bit."

Layla gave her sister a playful eye roll as Sofia slipped on her jacket and headed out the back door, the cold night air immediately rushing in. The door clicked shut behind her, and Layla locked it out of habit, staring at the darkness outside for a moment before turning back toward the living room.

The house felt larger with Sofia outside, but it was cozy, familiar. Layla wandered into the living room, her mind already shifting to thoughts of Felix coming over. She curled up on the couch with a blanket, listening to the faint hum of the heater as it kicked on.

She always found comfort in the quiet routines they had built in the house. Sofia out in the shed, working on bikes almost every night. Layla reading a book or watching TV, waiting for Felix to join her. They had both settled into their own rhythms, and it worked for them.

Outside, Sofia crossed the yard toward the detached shed,

her boots crunching against the gravel path. The shed was a decent size, more like a small workshop, and it was where she spent most of her free time. Tonight, she had Vince's Harley to work on, a tune-up he'd been pestering her about for weeks. She enjoyed the work, though—the solitude, the focus it required. It kept her hands busy and her mind quiet.

She pushed open the shed door and flicked on the overhead lights. The familiar hum of fluorescent bulbs greeted her as the space lit up, casting a stark contrast against the deep blackness outside. Sofia set down her tools on the workbench and rolled the bike over to the center of the shed, taking a deep breath as she surveyed her workspace.

Outside the shed, the world was a wall of darkness. The only light came from the house, a warm glow from the kitchen window and a dim front porch light, casting a faint circle around the steps. Beyond that, the surrounding fields and trees were swallowed by the night. It was always this way out here—isolated, quiet, peaceful.

Most nights, Sofia loved it. The darkness had become familiar to her, almost comforting. But tonight, for some reason, there was a strange stillness in the air, something that made her pause for just a moment before shaking it off.

"Alright, girl, let's get this done," she muttered to herself, grabbing her wrench and leaning over Vince's bike. The mechanical work always helped clear her mind, and within minutes, she was lost in the rhythm of adjusting the bolts, tightening the cables, and checking the engine.

Outside the shed, the night pressed in, silent and thick, but Sofia paid it no mind. This was her space, her world.

Back in the house, Layla was comfortably sprawled on the couch, fully absorbed in reruns of *Sons of Anarchy*. Smiling at the screen, she threw another grape into her mouth while the show's scene filled with gunfire and loud engines.

NINE

Sofia hummed softly to herself as she worked, the music playing quietly from her phone on the workbench. The steady rhythm of the song provided a comforting backdrop as she tightened the last bolt on the motorbike. The crickets outside blended with the music, and everything felt calm, normal. Layla's car was parked nearby, a familiar, reassuring presence.

She paused for a moment, wiping her greasy hands on her jeans, enjoying the satisfaction of a job well done. That's when the back sensor light flicked on, casting a sudden, bright glow through the shed's small window.

Her hands froze mid-motion. At first, she thought

nothing of it. "Oh, did you miss me, sis?" she called out, smiling slightly, expecting Layla's familiar teasing response. Silence. She waited, glancing toward the house, expecting to see Layla's silhouette pass the window. But there was no movement, and then it struck her—she hadn't heard the back door open or close.

Frowning, she turned back to the motorbike, but a strange sense of unease crept into her mind. Something felt... off. The crickets had gone silent. No distant night sounds. The air outside seemed unnaturally still.

She blinked and glanced at the window. Still, nothing stood out, but the nagging feeling that something was wrong wouldn't leave her. The music, once a pleasant distraction, now felt too loud. Slowly she reached over and turned off the music.

The shed fell into total silence.

Her pulse quickened as she strained to listen, her ears now attuned to every tiny sound. At first, there was nothing—just her own unsteady breaths and the pounding of her heart. She wanted to believe that the light had been triggered by a racoon or some other furry little critter, but she felt uncharacteristically anxious.

Then she heard it—footsteps. Heavy. Bipedal. Right outside the shed.

A silhouette passed by the window—tall, broad, inhuman. She started panicking.

She wanted to run, but her legs felt frozen. The footsteps stopped just outside the door. Sofia swallowed hard and stepped back, her eyes darting to the motorbike. She hoped it might shield her somehow, though she knew it wouldn't be enough.

The door rattled violently before exploding inward, sending splinters flying. Sofia's heart thundered as the creature barrelled through, its yellow eyes gleaming in the dim light. She stared at the monstrosity in front of her, everything else blurring into darkness except the creature.

It was massive, its towering form filling the doorway as it stood upright on two powerful legs. Dark, wild fur framed a face twisted in a way that seemed more monster than animal. Each breath brought a low, guttural growl from its chest, vibrating through the air. Long, razor-sharp claws caught the faint light as it stepped forward, every movement deliberate, inching closer, as if savoring her terror.

"Oh my God …," Sofia barely managed to mutter.

Without thinking, Sofia grabbed the closest thing she could—a wrench from the bench—and hurled it at the creature with all her strength. It struck its shoulder with a dull thud, but the creature barely flinched. Instead, it snarled, enraged.

Panic surged through her, and she darted toward Layla's parked car, diving beneath it. Her body scraped against the cold concrete as she tried to push herself as far underneath as possible. Tears started falling down her cheeks, her body trembling uncontrollably.

The creature roared, slashing at the ground with its massive claws, trying to reach her. Metal screeched as it raked its claws across the car's frame. Sofia stifled a cry, scooting further under the vehicle, her heart hammering in her chest.

For a moment, the creature's claws barely missed her leg, and she bit her lip, holding back a scream. Then, the sound of a car engine rumbled in the distance, headlights momentarily illuminating the shed through the window. The creature paused, its head snapping up, distracted by the approaching vehicle.

It growled low, agitated, before turning and sprinting off, leaving the shed in complete silence once more.

Sofia's limbs were shaking, but she knew she had to move. She crawled out from under the car, adrenaline propelling her forward. Her legs felt weak, but she sprinted towards the house, desperate to get there before the monster returned.

Layla got up from the couch and paused her show, frowning as she caught the sound of something outside. She took a few cautious steps toward the kitchen, listening carefully. Just as she reached the doorway, a loud bang rattled the back door, making her jump with a frightened gasp. Heart pounding, she froze, straining to hear any further sounds.

As she reached the door, she froze. Sofia's face appeared in the glass, pale and streaked with grease and blood. She was banging on the door, her eyes wide with terror, her lips moving in a silent plea.

"Sofia?" Layla whispered, as she ran to the door.

Then she saw it—the blood dribbling from Sofia's mouth and her eyes dilate. She gasped, hand flying to her throat.

Sofia slid down the door, her body crumpling to the floor. Behind her, the looming shadow of a creature appeared, its eyes locked on Layla.

The scream tore from Layla's throat as the creature slammed into the door, sending it crashing open. Sofia's limp body sprawled across the floor as the beast stepped over her, eyes burning with fury.

Layla bolted toward her bedroom, adrenaline flooding her veins. She slammed the door shut and threw herself against a heavy chest of drawers, trying to push it in front of the door. Her fingers dug in, nails ripping off under the strain as she struggled against the weight. Then, with a terrifying crack, the door began to splinter.

The creature's claws tore through the wood, shoving the door aside as it burst into the room. Layla backed into the corner, terror freezing her in place.

"No, no, no..." she screamed, her voice breaking, but the creature lunged with unstoppable force.

- - - - - - - - - - - -

An hour later, Felix pulled up in his truck, Layla's house looming quietly in the distance. Usually, a sense of calm washed over him when he arrived, but tonight, an uneasy tension lingered, though he couldn't quite place why. As he stepped out, he glanced at the shed where the light was still on but didn't see Sofia. Figuring she was inside, he continued into the house, calling out as he entered. The familiar warmth of Layla's presence was nowhere to be felt, and the silence hung heavy around him.

"Layla? Sofia?" His voice echoed, but the house was silent.

As he moved through the hall, the smell hit him—sharp, metallic, unmistakable. Blood. His chest tightened as his gut churned with unease. Something terrible had happened.

From where he stood, Felix could see down the hallway to the back door, barely clinging to its hinges, blood streaked across the floor in dark, violent smears. His heart thundered as his gaze locked on the crimson trail, the warmth and familiarity of Layla's home now gone, replaced by something cold and nightmarish.

He swallowed hard, panic rising as he stepped forward. There was no sign of a body, just the blood leading out into the night. His breaths came faster, his mind racing through the possibilities. But he didn't turn back. He couldn't—not with Layla and Sofia unaccounted for.

Felix's gaze swept through the house as he called out Layla's name, but only silence answered him. Then he saw her bedroom door, hanging open, a faint light spilling from within. Dread twisted in his gut, pulling him toward the room, though every instinct urged him to turn back.

With a shaky breath, he cleared some debris from his path

and stepped inside, bracing himself for whatever awaited him.

Layla's body—his Layla—was unrecognizable, torn apart in the corner of the room. Blood soaked the walls and bed sheets, and her face... her beautiful face... gone. Felix staggered back, collapsing against the doorway as the horror of it all crashed down on him.

His legs gave out, and he slid to the floor, his head spinning. A guttural cry escaped his throat, filled with disbelief and agony. Tears streamed down his face, and his hands shook as he reached out, as if he could somehow reverse the carnage before him. He choked on his sobs, overwhelmed by the grotesque sight of the woman he loved, slaughtered so brutally.

"No... no, no, no," he muttered, his voice breaking. "Layla..."

The grief was unbearable, ripping through him like the creature's claws. His mind refused to process it, as though this had to be some cruel nightmare. How could Layla be gone? How could she be reduced to this?

He crawled toward her, his fingers brushing the bloodstained floor, his soul screaming for her to wake up, to smile at him like she always did. But the reality of her mutilated remains was undeniable. It broke him. Felix cradled her head in his hands, sobbing, his whole body trembling with anguish.

For a long moment, all he could do was kneel there, overcome, his grief choking him with each ragged breath. In a daze, he reached for his phone, only to realize his hands were slick with blood. He wiped them hurriedly on his shirt, the action somehow grounding him enough to dial. When he finally managed to call 911, his voice came out in a hoarse whisper, barely audible through his choked sobs.

"9-1-1, what is your emergency?" The operator's voice was calm, professional.

"P-please... please, someone get here." His voice came out in fractured whispers. "It's Layla... she's gone. She's... oh God..." He broke off, the words dissolving into a harsh sob.

"Sir, can you tell me your location?" the operator asked gently. "I will send help, but we need the address."

Felix swallowed, squeezing his eyes shut to keep the grief from swallowing him whole. "Her house... it's... there's blood everywhere," he choked out. "I don't know what happened."

"Stay with me," the operator said, her tone soft but steady.

"Can you give me the address?"

He took another tremulous breath, forcing himself to focus. "314... Pinewood Drive," he whispered. "Please... please hurry."

"Help is on the way, sir," the operator assured him. "Can you stay on the line?"

Another sob tore through him, and he barely managed to whisper, "I... I can't look at her. Just... please, hurry..."

Felix stayed on the floor, shattered and broken, unable to move as the horrifying truth of what he'd seen sank deeper into his soul. The woman he loved, the life they were supposed to have together—it was all gone, brutally ripped away by the nightmare that stalked them.

TEN

Perry sat back in his worn recliner, the quiet hum of *Breaking Bad* reruns filling the room. It was late—too late for most folks to be awake—but as Chief Deputy, Perry was always on call, especially in a town like this. He took a sip of his lukewarm coffee, knowing sleep wouldn't come easily tonight, though he had no idea just how much worse this night was about to become.

The phone rang, cutting through the stillness. Perry's heart skipped a beat. Calls at this hour were rarely good news. He set his mug down and answered, trying to mask the tiredness in his voice.

"Chief Deputy Perry."

It was one of the younger deputies, his voice shaky, breath hitching. "S-sir, we… we've got a situation. There's been… an attack—the Vaughn sisters, out on the edge of town. I… I think you need to come out here."

Perry's stomach twisted. He knew the sisters, everyone did. This couldn't be happening. Not them.

"I'm on my way," Perry said, hanging up quickly. He grabbed his jacket from the hook by the door, then opened the drawer of the hallway table and pulled out his service weapon. Sliding it into the holster, he locked up and headed out to his cruiser.

Outside, the cool air and star-filled sky felt like a cruel contrast to the horror that awaited him. Perry climbed into his truck and sped toward the sisters' home, his mind a blur. He didn't know what he would find, but from the call, he knew one thing—it wasn't going to be good.

When Perry arrived at the property, he was greeted by the flashing lights of patrol cars and the low murmur of voices. Yellow crime scene tape fluttered in the light breeze, marking the perimeter. Quietly looming in the background, the house felt unsettling, even with its lights on.

He stepped out of the cruiser, and took a deep breathe

Several deputies were already on-site, their grim expressions telling him everything he needed to know. Something terrible had happened here—something they'd never be able to forget.

Perry approached one of the deputies standing near the driveway. "What are we looking at?" he asked, his voice calm but firm.

The young deputy, Daniels, stood ashen faced under the flashing lights, his eyes wide and haunted. He swallowed hard, struggling to find his voice. "I... I've got no words for this scene, Chief. Layla and Sofia... were good people. I can't believe it."

Perry's heart sank, but he kept his expression neutral. "What happened?"

"We're still figuring it out. It looks like... well, it looks like Layla was attacked by some sort of animal. It's brutal, Perry. She was mutilated... you need to see for yourself."

Perry nodded, though his stomach churned. He flashed back to the gruesome scene at the campground, how horrible it had been. He knew this one wasn't going to be any better—particularly as he knew the victims well. Taking another deep breath to steady himself, he walked toward the house.

The moment Perry stepped inside, the metallic smell of

blood hit him hard. Deputy Daniels, looking shaken, gestured toward the hallway. "In the bedroom," he muttered.

Perry took one look at Layla's crumpled body and had to steel himself against the bile rising in his throat. The cuts on her were deep and jagged, as if something had torn into her with savage intent. His gaze lingered on her neck, where bite marks and raw, torn flesh painted a gruesome picture. His stomach twisted, and he forced himself to take it in—to process the full brutality. Her face was missing. In its place was only an unrecognizable mass, pieces of flesh torn away as if a wild animal had ravaged her.

Perry averted his gaze, his mind in a whirl. "Sofia?" he asked quietly, already dreading the answer.

Daniels shook his head. "We haven't found her yet. There's a lot of blood near the back door, though."

Perry frowned. Sofia was strong—stronger than most people gave her credit for. But if Layla hadn't made it...

A call from outside broke the tension. "Chief, out here!"

Perry and Daniels rushed toward the back of the house, the beam of a flashlight illuminating a grim sight behind the shed. Sofia's body was there, half-hidden in the brush and weeds, her limbs twisted unnaturally. Blood pooled beneath her, dark and thick.

She had been dragged there—away from the house, and into the dark. It was clear to see she had been fed upon. Deputy Daniels struggled to keep his composure, his face pale as he stared at the ragged wounds and the pieces of flesh torn from her stomach.

Perry's hands clenched into fists, but he forced himself to remain calm. He had to stay in control.

The coroner, Doc Whitmore arrived not long after, a grim expression on his face as he surveyed the scene. Crime scene techs moved in, photographing every detail, cataloging the horror that had unfolded here. Perry watched them work, his mind already running through the possibilities.

After a while, Perry approached Doc Whitmore, who was inspecting Sofia's wounds with a practiced eye.

"You think it's the same animal?" Perry asked quietly.

Doc Whitmore didn't look up right away, his gloved fingers tracing the bite marks. "As the campground? I can't say for certain, not yet. But... these wounds—they're consistent with what we saw on the man yesterday. The bite marks, the cuts... it's likely."

Perry's stomach twisted. He'd hoped the campground attack was random, a one-time thing, but this—this was the work of something deliberate. Something that wasn't stopping.

"What about Layla?" Perry asked, his gaze drifting back toward the house.

Doc Whitmore hesitated before answering, his gaze shifting away momentarily. "Similar injuries," he said slowly, his tone carrying a hint of unease. "The cuts are deep and jagged, precise in some areas, savage in others. Whatever did this... it didn't just want to kill. It wanted to destroy."

He paused, as though weighing his next words, then added, "You know, in the preliminary autopsy of Tom... I noticed something odd about the bite marks. They're consistent with a wolf, but the size is... unusual. Exceptionally large. Bigger than anything I've seen before."

Perry's face tightened as he absorbed this. "So we're looking at something out there that's not just wild—but something powerful, too."

Doc Whitmore nodded gravely, folding his arms. "And something unlike any wolf we'd normally find in these parts. Whatever's doing this, it's... on a different scale."

Perry breathed out slowly, as he felt the gravity of the words envelop him. It was more than just a mere animal attack. It was a ruthless predator, cold and calculating, that had taken the lives of two more people.

"Make sure everything is documented," Perry said, turning to the deputies with a hard edge to his voice. "We need every piece of evidence we can get."

Hours passed as the crime scene team worked, the cold air pressing down on everyone, thick with the chill of dread. Perry stood back, watching as they finally loaded the bodies into the coroner's van.

A family member had come to collect Felix, who had been slumped in shock, his devastation almost too heavy for him to walk under as he was led to a car, sobbing uncontrollably.

Perry's eyes were on the scene, but his mind was miles away, processing everything that had happened in the last 24 hours. Sofia, Layla—two sisters, gone in one night. This wasn't just a tragedy; it was an escalation.

As the van pulled away, Perry felt a chill run through him, a premonition of more bloodshed. The sheriff wouldn't like it, but Perry knew he couldn't sit back this time. He was going to take the lead, come hell or high water. They couldn't afford to wait for another attack. They had to figure out what was stalking the outskirts of town—and they had to stop it before it claimed more lives.

ELEVEN

Perry sat at his desk, bleary-eyed and exhausted from the events of the previous night. The smell of stale coffee hung in the air, but it did little to keep him alert. He hadn't slept—not after what he'd seen at the sisters' house. His mind was a whirlwind of thoughts as he sifted through the crime scene reports, trying to make sense of the horror that had unfolded.

The door creaked open, and in waddled Sheriff Becan. His uniform strained against his gut, and his badge was half-hidden beneath the folds of his shirt. A sticky pink, sugary stain marked the front of his crinkled shirt, likely from a stop at the local bakery before coming in. Perry barely acknowledged him, but the sheriff gave a half-hearted nod and dropped into the chair across from him, his belly spilling over his belt.

Without saying a word, Becan pulled a crumpled cigarette from his pocket and lit it, ignoring the large "No Smoking" sign on the wall. Perry's eyes flicked toward the sign, the acrid smell of smoke curling through the room, stinging his nostrils. Becan either didn't care or pretended not to notice. More likely, he just didn't care.

"Heard you had a late one," Becan grumbled, his voice thick with sleep, as if being awake was an inconvenience.

Perry forced himself to stay calm, his frustration simmering beneath the surface. "Yeah. We need to talk about what happened."

Becan raised a lazy eyebrow, already looking bored. "Two girls, right? Sofia and Layla Vaughn, weren't they? Damn shame. Sofia was the best mechanic in town. Sounds like some kind of animal attack."

Perry clenched his jaw. This wasn't just an animal attack, and Becan knew it. "Sheriff, this is serious. Whatever attacked them isn't something we can just chalk up to a wild animal. The way they were torn apart, the bite marks... this thing is more dangerous than any bear attack. That's three dead in 24 hours."

Becan waved a dismissive hand and took a long drag of his cigarette. "Animals attack people sometimes, Perry. It's nature. No need to make it more than it is."

Perry's frustration grew. He felt a deep sense of responsibility for the town, a protectiveness that Becan would never understand. Becan was content to sit back and do nothing, and it infuriated him. "It's more than that. Layla and Sofia weren't just attacked—they were hunted. Sofia's body was dragged behind the shed and fed on. This thing isn't going to stop. We're not equipped to handle this."

Becan rolled his eyes and blew a cloud of smoke lazily toward the ceiling. "Look, Perry, I get it. It's nasty, but we don't need to be making waves. You start talking about bringing in outside help, and suddenly we've got the state, or worse, the feds, crawling all over this town. You think we need that? This town doesn't need attention. We'll handle it in-house."

Perry leaned forward, his voice steady but filled with barely contained frustration. "Sheriff, this goes beyond what our department can handle. If we don't act now, more people are going to die. We need more resources, more expertise. If you don't want to call the state, then call in wildlife experts or—"

Becan's eyes narrowed slightly, but it wasn't fear—it was annoyance. He took another drag, the cigarette ash growing long. "No. No outsiders in my town, Perry. Once they get their foot in the door, they start poking around, asking questions. Next thing you know, the Mayor's breathing down my neck. You don't need to worry about it."

Perry felt his blood boiling, but he kept his voice level. "The Mayor's already worried, sheriff. If more bodies turn up, he'll want answers, and if we don't have them, he'll go over your head. He doesn't want this town under the spotlight for doing nothing."

Becan smirked, flicking ash onto the floor with casual disdain. "The Mayor?" He chuckled. "I'll handle my brother-in-law, like I always do. He's not going to cause any trouble."

Perry's heart sank. The Mayor, the one person who could hold Becan accountable, was family. Of course Becan had no fear of the consequences.

Becan leaned forward, his gut pressing against the desk, his face red with irritation. "Careful, Perry. You're walking a fine line here."

Perry didn't flinch. "I'm just saying we can't ignore what's happening. People are dying. We can't pretend this is just some run of the mill animal attack."

Becan stubbed out his cigarette with unnecessary force, grinding it into the ashtray. "You think I don't know what's going on?" His voice rose defensively. "But this is my town, and I'm the sheriff. You remember that. I'll decide what needs to be done. You don't tell me how to run my department."

The tension in the room crackled, but Perry didn't back down. "I'm not trying to tell you how to do your job. But we can't sit back and wait for more bodies to pile up."

Becan stood, pointing his finger mere inches from Perry's face. "Listen here, Chief Deputy. You're not running the show. I am. No one's coming in from the outside. We'll handle it. And if you know what's good for you, you'll watch what you say."

Perry bit his tongue as Becan waddled toward the door, his footsteps heavy. Before leaving, Becan glanced back. "I'll handle the Mayor. You focus on what I tell you to focus on. Got it?"

Perry nodded, but his mind was already racing. He couldn't let this slide—people's lives were at stake. As the door clicked shut behind Becan, Perry leaned back in his chair, staring at the reports on his desk. Becan would never step up or be proactive, but Perry couldn't shake the feeling they were running out of time. If more bodies turned up, the town would be in chaos. And if the sheriff refused to act, Perry might have to make some hard decisions on his own.

TWELVE

Sheriff Becan drove his cruiser down the empty back roads, the morning sun just beginning to burn off the fog that clung to the fields. The window was down, letting in the cool air, though it did little to clear the stale stench of cigarette smoke that hung thick inside the car. His mind drifted, replaying the events of the last few days—the deaths, the town's murmurs, and Perry's constant pestering. It was getting harder to keep things under control.

His phone rang, pulling him out of his thoughts. He glanced at the screen—Ed. Becan sighed, already knowing what the Mayor would want. He grabbed the phone from the passenger seat and answered with a grunt.

"Yeah?"

"Becan, it's Ed," the Mayor said, his voice all business. "What's going on with those girls getting killed last night? People are starting to ask questions."

Becan frowned, eyes on the road. "Just a wolf, Ed. Nothing to worry about. We'll handle it."

"A wolf?" There was a pause, and Becan could almost see Ed pinching the bridge of his nose. "Look, we've already had the attack on that guy at the campsite, and now this? People are spooked, Becan."

Becan exhaled slowly, puffing on the cigarette dangling from his lips. "Yeah, and they'll keep getting spooked if you listen to every rumor they spread. You know how folks are around here—superstitious as hell. They're already talking like there's some kind of monster out there. It's just a wolf. No need to panic."

The Mayor's voice dropped a notch. "You sure about that? I heard it was brutal. People are saying it didn't look like an animal attack. Did you even see the scene?"

Becan rolled his eyes, taking another drag. "Of course I did, Ed. It was bad, I'll admit that. But wolves don't exactly tidy things up when they're hungry. I'll put a team together, we'll track it down, and take care of it. We'll tell everyone it's handled, and the whole thing will blow over."

There was another pause, then Ed spoke, his tone softening. "Look, you know I've got an election next year, Becan. I don't need this blowing up into something bigger. People are nervous, and if this gets out of hand, the press will start poking around."

Becan chuckled, shaking his head as the smoke drifted toward the cracked window. "Relax. I'll handle it. I'll organize a hunt, get the boys together, and we'll take care of this like we always do."

"That's what I needed to hear," Ed said, sounding relieved. "And Perry? He's not going to stir up any trouble, is he?"

Becan smirked. "Perry's fine. He's too straight-laced for his own good, but he knows his place. I've got him under control. Don't worry about him."

Ed laughed lightly on the other end. "Alright, as long as it stays handled."

Becan nodded as he rounded a bend in the road, his grip tightening on the steering wheel. "You won't have anything to worry about, Ed."

The line went dead, and Becan tossed the phone onto the passenger seat with a smirk. He wasn't worried about Ed, the town, or anyone. A dead wolf, a few hushed rumors, and everything would go back to normal.

He took another drag from his cigarette, watching the smoke lazily drift out the window. The town was his, and no one was going to take that away from him.

THIRTEEN

hief Deputy Perry's tires crunched over the gravel as he pulled into the parking lot behind the county coroner's office. The small, squat building seemed even more uninviting in the harsh light of the early afternoon, its whitewashed walls streaked with grime. Perry sighed as he stepped out of the cruiser, taking a moment to gather himself before heading inside.

Autopsies were always hard to deal with, but this one was worse. Layla and Sofia were young, well-known in town, and the brutal nature of their deaths was spreading fear like wildfire. And now, it was up to him to get some clarity on what exactly had killed them.

The antiseptic smell hit him the moment he entered, mingling with the clinical coldness of the coroner's office. Perry's stomach tightened as he walked down the hallway toward the autopsy room. He had seen enough violence in his career, but this case was starting to get to him in a way he hadn't expected.

Doc Whitmore stood over one of the bodies, his face lined with the exhaustion that came from decades of examining the dead. Perry greeted him with a nod, bracing himself for what he was about to hear.

"Doc," Perry said quietly, stepping up to the table.

"Chief Deputy," Whitmore replied, pulling off his gloves. "You'll want to see this."

Perry moved closer to the slab where one of the girls, Layla, lay under a sheet, her arm exposed. Deep, jagged gashes ran along her skin, the wounds stark against her pale flesh. Perry's breath caught, but he forced himself to focus.

"The claw marks are distinct," Whitmore began, his voice steady but grim. "I've seen plenty of animal attacks over the years, but this... this is different."

Perry frowned, leaning in for a closer look. "Different how?"

"For starters, these marks are deeper and wider than anything you'd expect from a wolf or even a large bear. The claws that did this were bigger, sharper. And the bite marks…" Whitmore hesitated, his expression hardening. "They're similar to a wolf's, but there's something off. They're larger—almost nine inches wide, more than twice the size you'd see on any North American wolf. And look here…" He pointed to the impressions on Layla's side. "It has additional teeth that a wolf wouldn't have, almost like extra serrated points designed for tearing flesh."

Perry's stomach turned as he examined the marks. "You're saying this creature's built to kill more brutally than any predator we've seen?"

Whitmore nodded, his tone darkening. "It's not just killing out of necessity. Look at the pattern of the wounds—the spacing of the bites and slashes. It's as though it's mauling them for sport, not food. The level of mutilation goes far beyond what we'd expect in a survival-driven attack."

Perry's gut tightened. "Are we dealing with the same creature that killed the man at the campsite?"

Whitmore pulled out photographs from the earlier case, showing the man's injuries. "The wounds match: same depth, same pattern. This thing didn't just attack to feed—it's almost… toying with its victims."

Perry ran a hand through his hair, feeling the magnitude of the situation deepen. "And it's escalating," he murmured. "This isn't just a predator. It's something that enjoys the kill."

Whitmore met his gaze, his expression grave. "Exactly. And, Perry, whatever this thing is—it's not going to stop."

Perry clenched his jaw, his thoughts spinning. He thanked the doc and left, but the words lingered in his mind—this wasn't just about survival for the creature. It was hunting for the thrill of it.

The drive to Layla and Sofia's home was heavy with tension. Doc Whitmore's words replayed over and over in Perry's mind. Hunting for sport. That detail changed everything. The idea of an animal that killed not out of hunger, but for enjoyment, was deeply unsettling. It meant the danger was far from over.

When Perry arrived at the house, the scene felt even more haunting in the light of day. The place was quiet now, stripped of the chaos that had filled it the night before. The memories of flashing lights, blood, and frantic searches were still fresh in his mind as he stepped out of his cruiser and made his way to the back of the house.

The shed stood near the house, its door hanging open, broken and splintered. Perry made his way around to the back, to where Sofia's body had been found—dragged from the back door of the house, her lifeless form torn apart. Dark stains of blood still marked the ground, the scene burned into Perry's mind, impossible to forget.

He moved cautiously, his eyes scanning the area until something caught his attention—a faint imprint in the soft dirt near the shed. Perry crouched down, squinting at the ground. Footprints.

His pulse quickened as he leaned closer, studying the prints. They looked like those of a wolf, but something was wrong—they were far too large. Much too large, he thought. Pulling out his phone, he snapped a few photos, setting his pen beside one of the prints for scale. The longer he examined them, the more disturbed he became.

The depth of the prints suggested a heavy creature, far heavier than any wolf he'd seen, and the size alone was startling. But it was more than that. The shape was almost humanoid, with long claws and an unusual alignment. And the positioning... it appeared as if this creature had been walking on two feet.

Perry stood up, his thoughts going wild. He'd seen similar

prints at the campground—footprints like these near the site where the man had been attacked. The female witness had described a massive wolf-like creature standing on four feet that killed her boyfriend. Whatever had torn through Layla and Sofia, whatever was out here stalking people, was unlike any predator he'd ever encountered.

This was no ordinary wolf.

Border: The forest loomed dark and still at the border of the property as Perry's eyes lingered on the trees. For a long moment, he stood there, staring into the tree line, half expecting something to stir. But the forest remained silent, the only sound the soft rustle of the breeze through the tree branches.

Perry took a deep breath, turning back toward the house. He had what he needed for now, but this investigation was far from over. If Doc Whitmore was right—and Perry had every reason to believe he was—then whatever was responsible for these deaths wasn't finished.

FOURTEEN

Perry stepped out of his cruiser, feeling the pressure in the air as he walked toward the sheriff's station. The unease that had been around for days got worse as the sun went down. He had just come from the sisters' home, the disturbing details from the coroner still fresh in his mind.

As soon as he entered the station, he realized something was different.

The place was buzzing with activity. Deputies were moving around, checking gear, making quiet preparations. A group of locals stood nearby, armed with rifles and shotguns, their faces grim. Perry's eyebrows shot up in surprise. This wasn't the usual disorganized mess that Sheriff Becan was known for. Something was happening.

Before he could process what was going on, Perry's attention was drawn to a woman near the front desk, pacing and raising her voice. He recognized her immediately—Angel Perez, the girlfriend of Tucker Leney. She had filed a missing person's report about him just a few days ago. Her voice echoed across the station, tight with frustration.

"Has anyone heard anything about Tucker yet? Anything at all?" she yelled at the deputy stationed at the front desk, her arms crossed as she anxiously tapped her foot.

Perry sighed and walked over, trying to ease the situation. "Angel," he called out, his voice calm. "We're still keeping an eye out for him."

Angel turned to him, her eyes wild with a mixture of fear and anger. "Perry, it's been six days! Tucker and Bo were supposed to be back by now. I haven't heard a thing! Do you know anything?"

Perry nodded, his expression serious. "I understand you're worried, Angel. We're doing everything we can to locate them. Do you have any idea where they were headed? Did Tucker mention anything before he left?"

Angel hesitated, then let out a breath. "He didn't say

much. Just that he was going to make enough money to pay off all our bills once he got back." She glanced around as if searching for more details in her memory. "But he did write down something... 'Norris' on a notepad right before he left. I don't know what it means. That's all I've got."

Perry raised his brow. "Norris? And that doesn't ring a bell to you?"

She shook her head. "No, but I'm scared, Perry. He hasn't turned up, and neither has Bo."

Perry thought for a moment, filing the name away. Something about it felt off, like it tied into the larger puzzle he was trying to piece together. "I'll look into it further tomorrow," he assured her, trying to calm her nerves. "In the meantime, stay by your phone. If you hear anything, let me know right away."

Angel gave a curt nod before heading out, frustration still evident in the way she walked. Perry turned back to the station, knowing this wasn't the last he'd hear about Tucker Leney and Bo Hopkins.

Before he could dwell on it further, Sheriff Becan's voice pierced through the air, loud and demanding. "Perry! We're heading out in a few. You're leading the team—get a move on!"

Perry blinked in surprise, looking toward the sheriff. The place was still buzzing with activity, and Becan—who rarely showed this much interest in anything—seemed to be taking the situation seriously for once. *What the hell?* Perry thought. He had expected Becan to dismiss the whole thing as usual, to downplay the danger and do the bare minimum. But this? This was new.

He made his way over, and Becan waved him over with a grunt. "We're putting together a hunt. The town's getting spooked, and the Mayor's breathing down my neck. We must put an end to whatever's out there."

Ah, Perry thought. *That explained it. The Mayor was involved. That's why Becan was finally showing some initiative— it wasn't about the brutal attacks. It was about keeping their reputation intact.*

Becan slapped him on the shoulder, a grin spreading across his face. "We've got three deputies, four local hunters, and myself. That's enough firepower to take down anything that crosses our path."

Perry's eyes shifted to the group of men gathering their weapons. The hunters were tough, experienced guys—locals who knew the woods better than anyone. They looked serious, prepared. He felt a flicker of hope that maybe, just maybe, this would lead somewhere.

"All right, let's head out," Becan said, his voice loud and commanding as he addressed the group. "We're tracking this thing tonight.

The group set off toward the trailhead in separate vehicles. Perry arrived first, stepping out of his truck and taking in the stretch of forest that loomed ahead, the darkness thickening as dusk faded into night. Soon the others pulled up, one after the other, until all stood assembled, their vehicles parked in a loose row along the gravelly trailhead.

Perry noticed the sheriff's bravado, but also noticed where Becan positioned himself. The sheriff wasn't leading the charge—no, he was more than happy to take up the rear of the group, letting Perry and the others do the heavy lifting. Typical.

"Perry's in charge tonight," Becan added, motioning toward him. "He knows these woods better than anyone, and he's got a level head. Follow his lead."

Perry nodded, accepting the responsibility. This was serious, and while Becan might see it as just another show of force to quiet the Mayor and the town, Perry knew the stakes were much higher.

"All right," Perry said, his voice calm as he addressed the group. "We'll move in pairs, stay within sight of each other. If anyone sees anything, don't engage alone. Call out. We stick together."

The men nodded in agreement, their eyes sharp and focused. They had come prepared—rifles, shotguns, ammunition. This wasn't a game to them. Perry could see the resolve in their faces. They knew something dangerous was out there, and they were ready to face it.

Becan, of course, took up the back of the group, his shotgun slung lazily over his shoulder as if he were out for a casual stroll rather than a hunt for a killer. Perry resisted the urge to say something. At least the sheriff had shown up, even if he was more interested in appearances than the actual danger.

"Let's move out," Perry said, his voice firm. The group turned on their flashlights, beams cutting through the night as they began their march into the woods. The usual sounds of the night had gone unnervingly quiet.

FIFTEEN

Glancing skyward, Perry observed dark clouds glooming threateningly, foreshadowing the imminent rainfall and intensifying the shadows in the already dim woods. The cool air felt heavy, thick with anticipation, and every step they took was followed by the muffled crunch of leaves beneath their boots.

Perry led the group, his eyes scanning the darkened trail ahead as his flashlight beam sliced through the night. Yet, its bright glow did little to dispel the growing sense of unease that lingered over the group. Behind him, Les, a seasoned local hunter, walked cautiously with his rifle at the ready, his expression tense.

They had been walking for over an hour now, and the forest seemed almost too quiet. No crickets, no owls—just the sound of their cautious footsteps and the occasional snap of a twig. The tension was unmistakable, and Perry could feel anxiety creeping in as they ventured deeper into the woods.

Les, breaking the silence, leaned in closer to Perry as they walked. His voice was a quiet murmur, but in the stillness of the night, it felt loud. "What exactly are we looking for out here, Perry?"

Without breaking stride or glancing back, Perry responded, his voice steady but low, "We're looking for a large wolf."

The simplicity of the answer seemed to unsettle Les. He frowned but didn't push the question further. A wolf? Les had hunted wolves before, but this didn't feel like an ordinary hunt. Something about the way Perry said it—without a trace of doubt or hesitation—made it clear that this was no normal wolf. And if the stories around town were true… well, none of them had encountered anything like this before.

The group moved in near silence, each man's eyes flicking back and forth between the trees, every crack of a branch or rustle of leaves making their hearts jump. The darkness had a way of playing tricks on you, especially when you knew something dangerous was lurking just beyond your sight.

After another half-hour of walking, Perry stopped abruptly, raising a hand to signal the others to halt. His flashlight beam flickered over the ground, highlighting an area where the earth had been disturbed. Footprints. The same kind they had found near the crime scene, only now, they were fresher. Perry crouched down, examining the prints more closely. The size of the print was massive, far too large for a normal wolf. He snapped a photo on his phone, using his pen for scale again, just like before.

"We're close," Perry muttered, more to himself than anyone else.

Les shifted nervously beside him, glancing over his shoulder as if expecting something to emerge from the trees. "How close?"

Perry didn't answer. Instead, he rose to his feet and motioned for the group to continue forward, deeper into the woods. Les stole a quick look at the footprint Perry had inspected as they continued walking. His eyes widened as he took in its size, much bigger than a typical wolf in Wyoming. He shot a look at Perry, but said nothing, the unease in his expression unmistakable.

The tension among the men continued to build, growing more intense with each step they took. The trees seemed to close in around them, their twisted branches reaching out like dark, skeletal fingers. The forest floor was uneven, and the light from their flashlights barely penetrated the thick underbrush.

Then came the sound.

A snap of a branch behind them.

All eight men froze in place, their eyes darting toward the source of the noise. Perry's hand instinctively went to the rifle slung across his chest. His heart was pounding now, and he could feel the adrenaline surge through his veins.

"What was that?" whispered one of the deputies, his voice shaky.

Perry held up his hand, signaling for silence. His ears strained to listen, his breath held as the group stood still, waiting for another sound.

There it was again—another snap, this time closer.

Les turned, his eyes wide with fear. "Something's following us," he whispered.

Perry's pulse quickened, but he kept his expression steady, concealing the urgency simmering within him. He raised a hand, gesturing for the group to tighten up, pulling them closer together.

They fell into a tighter formation, staying within arm's reach of each other as they moved forward. The only sounds their cautious steps and heavy, laboured breathing. Whatever was lurking, they weren't about to give it a chance to pick them off one by one.

As they walked, Perry's senses were on high alert. Every sound was amplified. The possibility that the creature they were hunting was now hunting them wasn't lost on him.

Then came another sound—closer this time, heavier. A low rustling in the bushes to their right.

Perry's flashlight swung in that direction, and for a moment, the beam landed on something large. His breath caught. The others raised their rifles, but before they could get a clear look, a herd of elk came crashing down the trail, clearly spooked. The massive animals barreled through the underbrush, their hooves pounding the ground like thunder, and the men had to leap out of the way to avoid being trampled.

"Jesus!" one of the hunters gasped, his voice breaking the silence as he scrambled to his feet.

Perry lowered his rifle slightly, his pulse still racing from the sudden burst of adrenaline. It wasn't what they were expecting, but the herd had been enough to send a shock of fear through the group.

The men exchanged nervous glances, some letting out shaky breaths. The elk had been a scare, but it was a reminder of how close they were to real danger. If they weren't careful, the next creature they encountered wouldn't just pass them by.

Perry took a deep breath, his nerves on edge. He had expected tension, but this was something else. The night was alive with the feeling of being hunted, and the creature they were tracking could be anywhere, silently observing them.

Another hour passed, and the forest seemed to stretch endlessly before them. The men, who had started the hunt sharp and focused, were now showing signs of fatigue. Their footsteps were slower, their eyes less vigilant. Perry could sense it—fatigue was setting in, and with it came a dangerous lack of focus.

Les stumbled slightly as they moved through a dense

thicket, catching himself on a tree. He muttered something under his breath, frustration and exhaustion clear in his voice. Perry glanced around at the rest of the group. The adrenaline that had carried them through the first few hours was fading fast, and the men were growing weary. Tired men in the woods, carrying weapons and searching for a creature that could be anywhere, wasn't a good combination.

Perry's gaze settled on the sheriff. He looked worse for wear—sweat soaked through his shirt, and his breathing was labored. The sheriff wiped his forehead with the back of his hand, his exhaustion more evident with each passing minute. He wasn't just tired—he was nearing his limit, and Perry could see it.

Perry made a quick decision. He had intentionally looped them back closer to the trailhead as a precaution, knowing the risks of pushing too deep into the woods at night. They weren't too far off from the main trail now, which made his decision easier.

He raised a hand, signaling the group to stop.

"We're heading back," Perry said, his voice cutting through the quiet night. The men looked at him, some surprised, others relieved. "We've been out here long enough. You're all tired, and tired men make mistakes. Let's head back and get some rest."

There were no arguments. The anxiety, the fear, and the hours of tracking had worn them down.

The group made their way back to the trailhead, flashlights cutting through the darkness. There was a bit more energy in their steps now, knowing the hunt was coming to an end. Though the air still felt thick with the presence of something unseen, Perry kept his focus on getting everyone back safely. The creature was still out there, but tonight wasn't the night they would find it.

The men were quiet as they reached the trailhead, their exhaustion evident in the slow, heavy way they moved. Perry scanned the woods one last time, aware that the real danger was still out there, lurking, waiting for the right moment. He turned to the group and nodded, his voice unwavering despite the weariness in his own bones. "Thanks for coming out tonight," he said, his gratitude sincere.

As the men gathered their gear, Perry noticed the sheriff already in his truck, the engine roaring to life. Without a word, the sheriff was driving off, disappearing down the dirt road before anyone else had even started their vehicles.

SIXTEEN

es stifled a yawn, his heavy eyelids gripping the steering wheel tightly as he drove down the dark, winding road home. The hunt had unsettled him more than he cared to admit. All they'd been looking for was a large wolf—at least that's what Perry had said, and that's what they all believed. A wolf that had attacked the sisters and killed the camper.

Something about that explanation didn't sit right with Les. He shook his head, thinking of the footprint's sheer size. He'd hunted his fair quota of predators in these woods, but he'd never seen a track like that. The whole time he was out there, an uneasy feeling lingered—like they were chasing something far more dangerous than any animal he'd encountered.

Now, with the road stretching out before him and the strain of the long search heavy on his mind, he felt it even stronger—a sense of impending doom.

He had only four miles to go before he reached his house, but it felt like an eternity. His wife and child were there, likely fast asleep by now, blissfully unaware of the terror lurking just outside their walls. A large wolf? Maybe. But Les knew, deep down, that whatever was out there, it wasn't just any wolf. The feeling in his gut told him so.

Pulling in, his headlights illuminated the front of his house, casting a warm glow.

Just as he neared the house, something darted across the driveway in front of him. It was so fast that Les barely registered it, just a blur of motion.

"What... in the hell," Les muttered as he slammed on the brakes, his heart pounding wildly. The truck skidded to a stop, and for a long moment, he sat there, frozen, trying to make sense of what he had just seen.

"Get a grip, Les," he whispered, running a trembling hand through his hair. *"You're just spooked from the hunt... it was probably just a black bear. Yeah, a black bear."* He forced a deep

breath, his fingers gripping the steering wheel so tightly they ached. But no matter how hard he tried to convince himself, the knot of dread in his gut wouldn't ease. He knew whatever he'd seen wasn't just a bear.

"Just breathe. Just breathe," he repeated to himself as he closed his eyes.

The night around him was suddenly too quiet. No wind, no crickets—nothing. Just the sound of his irregular breathing and the pounding of his heart. Les swallowed hard, his eyes darting to the house. His wife, Laney, and their child were inside. He felt a surge of panic wash over him. Whatever was out here, it wasn't just a threat to him—it was a threat to his family.

For a few minutes, he sat there, gripping the steering wheel, his mind a blur. It was just a bear, he tried to convince himself, but the nagging sense of dread told him otherwise. Something else is out there. Something far worse.

Just breathe. Just breathe.

After what felt like hours, Les made a decision. He couldn't sit in the truck all night. He had to get inside, had to make sure Laney and his boy were safe. He grabbed the shotgun from the passenger seat, his hands trembling slightly as he double-checked it was loaded. The cold metal of the gun was a small comfort, but it wasn't enough to shake the overwhelming feeling of anxiety.

You've got this old boy, you've got this.

Slowly, he opened the car door, the creak of the hinge unnaturally loud in the stillness. Les stepped out, the cool air biting at his skin as he scanned the driveway and the surrounding woods. The air felt thick, suffocating.

"Get outta here," he called into the night, trying to steady his voice. "I've got a gun, and I ain't afraid to use it!"

Clutching the shotgun tightly, he moved carefully towards the porch, his words lingering in the air.

Every few steps, Les glanced over his shoulder, his eyes darting left and right for any sign of movement. The hair on the back of his neck prickled—a primal instinct warning him that something was very, very wrong.

When he finally reached the porch, his heart was pounding so hard he could hear it in his ears. He placed one foot on the bottom step, preparing to climb up, when suddenly, it hit him.

Like a freight train.

Something massive slammed into him from the side, knocking the wind from his lungs and sending him crashing to the ground. His shotgun flew from his hands, skidding across the porch as Les struggled to comprehend what had just happened. Pain exploded through his body as he hit the ground, and in the split second before he could react, he felt the claws.

Sharp, jagged claws tore into his back and side, ripping through his clothes and flesh with brutal efficiency. Les screamed, the sound primal and filled with terror, as the weight of the creature pinned him to the ground. He could feel its hot breath on his neck, hear the low growl rumbling from deep within its chest.

Just as the creature was about to deliver another vicious bite, the porch light flicked on. The sudden flood of light startled the beast, and Les heard a scream—Laney's scream—from the doorway.

The creature hesitated for a split second, its glowing eyes turning toward the light, before it released Les and bolted into the forest, disappearing as quickly as it had appeared.

Laney rushed to her husband's side, tears streaming down her face as she knelt beside him. Les was bleeding badly, his body torn from the attack, but he was alive. Barely.

"Les! Les, oh my God!" Laney cried, her voice trembling as she rushed to his side. "What in the hell was that thing?"

Les could barely respond, the pain overwhelming, but he managed a weak nod. Not wanting to stay out in the open a minute longer, Laney helped him to his feet, practically dragging him inside the house. Once inside, she locked the door and eased him onto the couch, where he collapsed face down.

Her hands shaking, Laney quickly pulled out her phone and dialed 911. While speaking to the operator, she grabbed some towels from the nearby cabinet and pressed them against the wounds, desperately trying to stem the bleeding.

The next few minutes were a blur for Les, his vision hazy and his strength fading. He could hear Laney's frantic voice, full of fear, as she relayed their situation. And then, faintly, the sound of approaching sirens cut through the night, growing louder as the ambulance and law enforcement rushed toward their home.

By the time Chief Deputy Perry arrived, the paramedics were already loading Les into the ambulance. His body was wrapped in thick bandages, but the extent of his injuries was clear—dislocated shoulder, deep gashes, shredded skin, and blood soaked through his bandages. Perry's face hardened as he approached Laney, who was standing on the porch, her face pale and tear-streaked.

"What happened?" Perry asked, in a quiet and urgent voice.

Laney shook her head, still in shock. "It... it attacked him. That thing... it was gonna kill..."

She couldn't finish the sentence, her voice breaking as she sobbed.

Perry glanced toward the forest, his eyes focused. He had hoped they were done with this for the night, that the hunt had driven the creature away. But now, seeing the devastation it had wrought on Les, he knew the truth.

This wasn't something they could handle alone.

Perry took out his phone, his determination clear as he dialed the number. His tone unwavering but urgent, he said, "This is Chief Deputy John Perry in Enrick, Wyoming." "We need federal assistance—immediately."

As he hung up, Perry lingered on the porch, staring into the dark woods, half-expecting to see eyes glinting back at him—watching, waiting. Relief washed over him knowing help was on the way, but he could only hope whoever they sent would be ready for what they were up against.

SEVENTEEN

The Dogman burst into the thick woods, its breath ragged from the sprint away from the light. Its heart still pounded from the attack, and the taste of the man's blood lingered on its tongue. But the sudden flare of brightness had sent a shock through its system, spurring a primal fear that drove it deeper into the forest.

The hunger clawed at it again, and the Dogman sniffed the air, searching for prey. It caught the scent of a deer nearby and crept toward it. The deer grazed peacefully, unaware of the predator lurking just out of sight. In a swift, lethal strike, the Dogman lunged, claws sinking into the animal's side, bringing it down. The kill was quick, efficient, but as it tore into the flesh, there was no sense of satisfaction. It ate only because it had to, yet the emptiness remained.

After finishing, the Dogman slunk back into the shadows and found a concealed spot among the trees to rest. It curled up, licking the blood from its claws, but sleep wouldn't come. Its mind wandered back to the memory it couldn't escape: the sight of its younger sibling, lifeless and trapped, left behind. It had been his responsibility to look after her, and he had failed. If the pack ever found out, they would cast him out, or worse. He knew he would never be able to return to them.

A low growl rumbled in its throat as it curled tighter, loneliness and guilt mingling with the sharp edge of hunger. The humans it hunted now weren't prey for survival—they were reminders of his failure, marks of vengeance against a world that had taken everything from him. It ate to satisfy the overwhelming hunger and killed out of a thirst for revenge. But no matter how many lives it took, the guilt never faded.

EIGHTEEN

Early the next morning, the missing person report for Tucker Leny lay open on the desk, surrounded by scattered notes and files. Perry gave his word to Angel Leney that he would personally look into Tucker's disappearance. Tucker and his closest companion Bo had been missing for a week, and now the pressure was building. Les's attack the night before continued to haunt him, but today he was resolved to dig a little deeper into what happened to them.

On the computer screen, Tucker's criminal history stretched back to his teenage years. Multiple arrests—drug charges, a few burglaries—he'd done a few short stints in jail, but there were no active warrants and nothing to suggest he'd suddenly vanish. Whatever had happened, this wasn't about Tucker running from the law.

Perry's gaze drifted to the section of Tucker's history that stood out more than the others: his brother's death. Tucker had been just 17 when his older brother died in a car wreck that had rocked the entire town. Four teens had lost their lives that night, including Tucker's brother, and it had been big news. The tragedy had left a scar on the Leney family, and Tucker had never been the same since. Some said the loss was what sent him down a troubled path. But even with all that, he wasn't the type to just vanish without a trace.

He scrolled through Tucker's records again, searching for any link he might've missed, but nothing added up. The quiet in the station felt suffocating, a constant reminder that time was slipping away.

A thought flashed across Perry's mind: could the creature be connected to the disappearances of Tucker and Bo? The timeline fit. Maybe they had been attacked first, before the camper. The unsettling possibility lingered—a connection he couldn't ignore, especially considering how much time those two had spent within the forest.

Before he could delve deeper into the thought, the sharp, echoing sound of a door slamming open jolted him from his reverie.

Perry barely had time to react before Sheriff Becan stormed into the room, his face flushed with anger. Without a word, the sheriff slammed his hand down on Perry's desk, hard enough to send papers fluttering across the surface.

"What on earth, Perry?" Becan yelled, his voice filled with rage. "Who gave you the authority to contact the feds? Huh? Who told you to do that?"

Perry didn't flinch, though his heart rate quickened. He had expected this confrontation, but not quite so soon. Becan loomed over him, encroaching on his personal space, his eyes filled with rage. Still, Perry held his ground.

"I did what needed to be done," Perry replied calmly, though there was steel in his voice. "After Les Fay was attacked last night, I couldn't just sit around and pretend we've got this under control. You know we don't. We need more resources, more people—"

"More people?" Becan cut him off, his voice rising. "More attention, you mean! You've brought the feds down on us, Perry! This is my town! No-one gave you the authority to contact them! You're a damn fool, boy!"

Perry's hands clenched into fists under the desk. "Les was

nearly killed, sheriff! That thing's out there, and we can't handle it alone. We need help, and you know it. We can't just sit here while more people get torn apart. I couldn't live with that on my conscience."

Becan's eyes flashed with anger. "I don't give a damn about your conscience, Perry! You've ruined everything. You think I want the feds crawling all over this town, asking questions, bringing in the press? You've put us in the spotlight, and for what? You've embarrassed me in front of the Mayor. He just got off the phone with me—he's pissed, Perry! Pissed!"

Perry could feel the tension mounting, but he wasn't backing down. "What do you want me to do, sheriff? Sit back while this thing keeps killing? You can pretend all you want, but we're not equipped for this. You know it, and I know it. We needed help."

Becan slammed his hand down again, his face inches from Perry's. "I should fire you right now. Do you hear me? You went behind my back, undermined my authority—"

"I did what was necessary," Perry shot back, standing up from his chair, his voice rising. "This isn't about your authority, sheriff. This is about saving lives. You can stand there and throw a fit all you want, but that thing out there? It's not stopping. And unless we do something about it, more people are going to die. Les barely survived, and next time it might be someone else. Someone we can't save."

Becan paused, Perry's words seeming to sink in, though his face remained flushed with anger. A vein pulsed on his forehead as he paced the silent room, the unease between them thickening with each step.

"You've crossed the line, Perry," Becan said quietly, his voice deadly calm. "You've made a mess of this, and now I'm the one who has to clean it up. The Mayor wants your head for this, and don't think I'm not considering it. You've embarrassed me, and you've embarrassed this department. You better hope the feds don't make things worse."

Perry straightened his shoulders, refusing to let Becan's words shake him. "If calling in the feds saves lives, then it's worth it. You can be angry all you want, sheriff, but at the end of the day, we need help. That's what matters."

Becan glared at him for a long moment, his hand still gripping the edge of the desk. Finally, he pushed himself away, turning his back on Perry as he stormed out of the office, slamming the door behind him.

Perry rose to his feet, exhaling slowly as the adrenaline dissipated. The confrontation had been inevitable, but it didn't make it any easier. He knew what he had done was right, but Becan was still the sheriff, and the consequences of going behind his back were far from over.

But deep down, Perry didn't regret a thing. They needed help—help that was now on the way. Whatever it took, he was ready to face the fallout, because he knew the alternative was far worse.

NINETEEN

The jet's wheels screeched against the tarmac as Special Agent Nicole Beretti's plane touched down at Cheyenne Regional Airport. She exhaled and leaned back in her seat, feeling the jet slow to a stop. Primarily serving the nearby F.E. Warren Air Force Base, Cheyenne Regional saw more military traffic than civilian flights. The airport had a no-nonsense, utilitarian feel—much like the people who passed through it.

Beretti gathered her bag and made her way to the exit, her mind spinning back to the urgent call from ASAC Nathan Ward. She had been asleep in a hotel in Illinois when the phone rang, still groggy and disoriented, but Ward's voice had come through the phone sharp and clear, his tone leaving no room for hesitation.

The minute she heard his voice, she knew it was urgent. Ward had trusted her with the most dangerous cases in the field. This one was no different.

As she stepped off the plane, Beretti scanned the tarmac, and there by the black SUV stood Special Agent Noah Jacobi. He was a solid 6'2", well-built with the kind of rugged look that spoke to someone who had seen his share of tough situations. His goatee, neatly trimmed, added to his sharp appearance, and his closely shorn brown hair framed a friendly smile that softened his otherwise tough exterior. He looked up as Beretti approached, a flicker of recognition crossing his face.

"Beretti," Jacobi called, pushing off the car and extending his hand. His tone was professional, but there was relief in his eyes. He was clearly glad to see her.

"Noah," Beretti replied, shaking his hand firmly. "Good to see you. Alabama, right?"

Jacobi nodded, his smile faint. "Yeah, Alabama. Fort McClellan. Hard to forget that one."

Beretti gave a small nod, recalling the assignment vividly. "Sasquatch on a military training facility. That was a mess."

Jacobi chuckled, though the memory wasn't exactly a fond one. "Tell me about it. We barely made it out of there. Never thought I'd be chasing down a cryptid on a decommissioned base."

Fort McClellan, now used as a training facility, had been a quiet place—until it wasn't. Their team had been called in after reports of strange sightings and the disappearance of a few soldiers. When they arrived, it became clear something big was lurking in the forests surrounding the base. The Sasquatch had terrorized the place, leaving chaos in its wake. It had taken every bit of their training to deal with it, but they had gotten the job done.

"That squatch was one tough son of a bitch," Beretti mused as they climbed into the SUV.

Jacobi nodded, a grim look crossing his face. "Oh yeah. I still have the scars to prove it."

As they got into the car, the road stretched out before them, and Beretti settled into the passenger seat, listening as Jacobi began the rundown of the case.

"It started about a week ago. The first attack was a camper—a guy had been hiking with his girlfriend and was attacked in their camp. Mauled and fed upon. Thankfully, the girlfriend escaped by scaling a tree. At first, the local sheriff thought it was a wolf or a bear, but the bite marks didn't match anything they've seen. The attack was vicious—more than a known animal would do. And it wasn't clean. Whatever did this... it tore him apart."

Beretti nodded slowly, listening carefully.

"Then, two sisters were found dead in their house, mutilated. Claw and bite marks everywhere. One of the sisters was dragged out of the house and fed upon behind a shed. Same pattern—too large for a wolf, too violent for a bear. Sheriff Becan tried to keep it quiet, but after the third incident... well, it couldn't be ignored and a Chief Deputy John Perry stepped in and called for help."

Beretti glanced at him, raising an eyebrow. "Wait—the sheriff's last name is Becan?"

Jacobi nodded, then laughed when he realized. "Oh! Spelled B-e-c-a-n, but I bet he's been catching hell since the day he pinned on that badge."

Beretti laughed. "I bet."

"Anyway, last night, a guy named Les Fay was attacked on his own porch," Perry said. "He'd just gotten back from a hunt the sheriff had organized to track the creature. His wife found him mid-attack, mauled by something she described as 'a cross between a Hollywood werewolf and a hyena.' She heard Les' screams and when she turned on the porch light it spooked the thing enough to take off before it could finish him. Les is in rough shape, but he will live. Whatever that thing was—it may have followed him home."

Beretti sat back, processing the information. Three confirmed attacks, one survivor. "And what are we looking at? Dogman?"

Jacobi secured his grasp on the steering wheel. "It's the likely culprit. Along with Les's wife's description, the female survivor from the campsite reported the same—wolf-like, fast, and incredibly large. The claw and bite marks point to something far bigger than any wolf typically found in Wyoming."

Beretti's mind flashed back to Hickory, Missouri. She had just come off a case dealing with two Dogmen that had terrorized the rural community. The brutality had been similar—excessive violence, prey not just hunted but mutilated. The pattern was familiar, and it didn't sit well with her.

"We could be dealing with a cryptid," she said finally. "If it's a Dogman, it won't stop with just a few attacks. This thing will escalate. The longer it goes unchecked, the more aggressive it'll get."

Jacobi shook his head, his jaw tight. "That's what I'm afraid of. Sheriff Becan doesn't want any outside help, but the situation is getting out of control. And as I said, the call for help didn't even come from him—it came from his Chief Deputy."

Beretti raised an eyebrow. "The Chief Deputy went over his sheriff's head?"

Jacobi nodded. "Yeah, that's the part that surprised me too. I guess Perry couldn't sit around and watch things get worse."

"Interesting," Beretti mused, glancing out the window. "That says a lot about the sheriff's leadership—or lack thereof."

Jacobi grimaced. "Maybe the sheriff's trying to keep people calm, but the town's on edge—understandably. He didn't want the feds involved, but Perry went behind his back and called it in after Les was attacked. Word is, the Mayor's not happy, and neither is Becan."

Beretti smirked. "They never are. But we're not here to make friends. We're here to solve a problem."

The road stretched on as they neared Enrick, a mix of anxiety and excitement hanging in the air. Beretti stayed composed, but her mind was already ticking through possibilities. She knew there was always a reason when a cryptid started attacking humans—normally, they kept their distance. Something had changed, something had driven this creature to cross that line.

And if this was a Dogman, they were going to have to act fast.

Breaking the silence, Jacobi spoke again. "We will introduce ourselves at the sheriff's office and then go to the hotel."

Beretti nodded, "Sounds good."

TWENTY

Perry stood at his desk, the sting of the sheriff's words still fresh in his mind. Pushing the confrontation aside, Perry focused on what needed to be done. Tucker Leney had been missing for over a week, and time was running out. If anyone knew where Tucker might've gone or what he'd gotten himself into, it would be his friends.

Grabbing his jacket, Perry decided to start asking questions. Tucker had a couple of close friends he'd been seen with before disappearing. It was as good a place as any to start.

The dive bar sat on the edge of town, its neon sign flickering weakly against the late morning sun. Perry pulled up, noting two vehicles parked outside—one was the bar owner's, and the other was a beat-up old pickup, caked in mud and rusted along the edges. It was unmistakably Brady Clemons' truck, the kind of worn-down ride typical of a country boy who'd seen his fair share of back roads.

Brady, one of Tucker's closest friends, was known for his early (or late) bar habits.

As Perry pushed open the door, the smell of stale beer and smoke hit him. Inside, the bar was dimly lit, with only the faint hum of the jukebox filling the silence.

Brady was hunched over the counter, nursing a beer at 11 a.m. His scruffy appearance and bloodshot eyes suggested he hadn't had much sleep.

Perry slid onto the stool next to him. "Brady."

Brady turned, squinting as if Perry's presence were somehow offensive. "Ch-Chief Deputy Perry," he mumbled, words blending together. "What brings ya here… to this niiice est-ab-lishment?"

"Looking for Tucker," Perry replied, ensuring his voice remained steady. "His girl hasn't seen him in over a week. I thought you might know where he's hiding."

Brady gave a dry laugh, taking a long, sloppy sip of his

beer. "T-Tuck... he's got his... ya know, his secrets," he muttered, trailing off. "Him an' Bo... they was up t'somethin'." He shook his head, glancing away like he didn't want to continue.

Perry leaned in, his gaze steady. "Up to what, Brady?" he pressed.

Brady grunted, avoiding eye contact, his fingers tapping on his beer. "Dunno, man. Tuck jus'... said he got in too deep. Wanted out, but... but couldn't figure it." He frowned, looking down into his glass. "Guess... guess Bo dragged him deeper 'n he wanted."

Perry narrowed his eyes. "Did he tell you who they were dealing with?"

Brady shook his head, swaying slightly. "Nah. Kept it... tight-lipped, y'know? All I know is... Tuck didn' trust them. Not one bit."

Perry knew he wasn't getting much more from Brady in his current state. "If you hear anything, you call me."

Brady raised his glass in a sloppy salute, his eyes unfocused. "Shhhure thing, Chief," he mumbled, tipping the beer back for another sip.

Next, Perry headed to the gas station on the outskirts of town, where another of Tucker's friends, Eddie Morrow, worked. Unlike Brady, Eddie was the quiet type—reliable, the kind of guy Tucker might confide in when things got messy.

Perry stepped inside, greeted by the hum of refrigerators and the smell of cheap coffee. Eddie was behind the counter, stocking cigarettes. He looked up as Perry approached, surprised to see him. "Chief Deputy Perry," Eddie greeted, standing up straight. "Something I can help with?"

"I'm looking for Tucker," Perry replied. "I already talked to Brady, but he didn't know much. I was hoping you could fill in a few gaps."

Eddie's face tightened, a flicker of discomfort crossing his expression. "I haven't seen him for a week or two," he admitted, his voice low. "Last time I saw him he was excited about a pay day. He wasn't one to keep quiet when he was on a roll."

Perry frowned. "Did he give any hint about who he and Bo were tangled up with?"

Eddie shook his head, clearly uneasy. "No, he clammed up anytime I asked. He did hint that they were in too deep but he couldn't say no to money."

Perry processed the information.

"If you hear from him, call me immediately," Perry said, handing Eddie his card.

Eddie nodded, tucking the card away. "Will do."

TWENTY-ONE

Beretti and Jacobi stepped through the doors of the sheriff's office, immediately sensing the friction in the air. The small-town station had the usual decor—a worn-out flag in the corner, a few plaques on the wall, and a coffee machine that looked like it might require police backup just to get a cup. But it was the atmosphere that Beretti picked up on first, the kind of unease that came with a power struggle.

Sheriff Becan stood with arms crossed, his eyes narrowed in displeasure as the two agents approached. His rumpled uniform looked as if he'd yanked it from a pile, and stubble darkened his face, evidence he hadn't bothered to shave in days. He looked exactly like the kind of sheriff Beretti had seen too many times before—there for the badge and title, but not the work of keeping the town safe. His whole demeanor exuded a deep-seated laziness, an air of indifference hanging around him like stale smoke.

Standing next to him was Chief Deputy Perry, who looked far more alert. His eyes shifted between Beretti and Jacobi with a quiet urgency, like he'd been waiting for them. Tall and wiry, Perry's frame spoke to a life of activity, and his clothes were neat and pressed, giving him a sharp, disciplined presence that stood in stark contrast to the sheriff's dishevelled look. While Becan seemed worn down, Perry looked as though he bore the burden of the department's shortcomings on his own shoulders, taking the town's safety as his personal responsibility.

"Sheriff Becan, Chief Deputy Perry," Jacobi greeted as they approached, extending his hand. "I'm Special Agent Noah Jacobi, and this is Special Agent Nicole Beretti."

Perry shook Jacobi's hand firmly, then turned to Beretti, offering her the same respectful handshake. "Welcome to Enrick," he said, his voice steady and sincere.

Beretti nodded, meeting Perry's gaze with appreciation before shifting her focus to the sheriff.

Becan, however, didn't extend a hand. Instead, he kept his arms crossed, his expression hard. "So, you're the Feds they sent us," he muttered, barely hiding his skepticism.

Jacobi gave a small, polite nod. "That's right."

"I didn't ask for you," Becan muttered, his voice quiet and thick with irritation.

Beretti's eyes flicked to Perry, catching the brief look of discomfort on his face. So, this was it. Becan wasn't just unimpressed by their presence—he was outright hostile to it. She'd been in situations like this before, where the local sheriff resented outside help, but this felt more personal. He didn't like that his own deputy had gone over his head.

"No, you didn't," Jacobi said evenly. "But Chief Deputy Perry thought it was necessary."

The sheriff's eyes darkened as he shot a look at Perry. "Yeah, well, maybe Perry's been overreacting a little."

"Sheriff," Perry began, his voice tense but controlled, "I called them in because this situation is beyond what we can handle alone. We've lost 3 people in the past week and only last night a good man nearly died. We need their help."

Beretti watched the exchange quietly, noting how Becan's

mouth twitched as if he wanted to argue but knew he couldn't. He was the kind of man who liked being in control, who probably used his title as sheriff to intimidate or avoid real work. She had met plenty of sheriffs like him—content to sit behind a desk and wear the badge, but unwilling to get their hands dirty. Men who valued the power but not the responsibility.

"So," Becan said, shifting his weight and crossing his arms tighter with a grunt. "What's the plan? You two gonna come in here and fix everything for us?"

Jacobi remained calm, unfazed by the sheriff's attitude. "We're here to assess the situation and offer assistance. Once we've reviewed all the evidence and discussed it further with Chief Deputy Perry, we'll come up with a plan."

Becan smirked, clearly unimpressed. "Right. Because I'm sure your 'plan' will fix everything."

Beretti shifted slightly, folding her arms as she spoke up for the first time. "We're not here to take over, sheriff. We're here because there's a real threat to the townsfolk. Whether you want to acknowledge it or not, people are dying. And unless something is done, it's going to get worse."

The sheriff scowled, but didn't say anything. Perry,

however, gave a slight nod of approval at Beretti's words. He knew the town's safety was at risk, even if his boss didn't want to admit it.

Perry cleared his throat, stepping in before the conflict could escalate further. "I've compiled everything we have so far—the reports on the attacks, witness statements, and photos of the crime scenes. You'll see that the evidence points to something... well, something we're not equipped to deal with."

Beretti and Jacobi exchanged a glance. They already knew what they were dealing with—cryptid attacks, most likely a Dogman. But they needed to see the evidence firsthand before moving forward.

"We'll review the evidence at the hotel and reach out once we've gone through everything," Jacobi said.

Perry nodded, walking over to a nearby filing cabinet and pulling out a thick folder. He handed it to Jacobi, who flipped through it briefly before tucking it under his arm.

"Appreciate your help on this," Perry said.

"No problem. I hope we can get this sorted before anyone else gets hurt," Beretti replied, her tone professional.

Becan grunted, waving a hand dismissively. "Fine. Do whatever you need to do. Just don't bring the media down on this town."

Beretti raised her eyebrows but said nothing. She wondered if the sheriff's annoyance was just a cover for something deeper. Why was he so against the feds being involved? It felt like more than just pride—maybe he was hiding something. She would file that thought away for later.

"We'll keep it discreet," Jacobi replied.

As they turned to leave, Jacobi couldn't help but feel a surge of frustration. They had a job to do, and it didn't matter whether the sheriff liked it or not. What mattered was stopping the attacks—and they were just getting started.

TWENTY-TWO

As soon as the door closed behind Beretti and Jacobi, Sheriff Becan let out an exaggerated sigh. He didn't even bother pretending to be interested in what was happening next. The moment those two feds walked out, he was done. He had no intention of sticking around and playing nice with them any longer than necessary.

Reaching for his phone, Becan grabbed his jacket and headed for the door, muttering under his breath. He walked briskly to his car, the scowl on his face deepening with every step. Once inside the vehicle, he wasted no time dialing the Mayor.

The phone rang twice before the Mayor's familiar voice

came on the line. "Becan, what's going on? You've got those agents there now?"

Becan grunted in response. "Yeah, they just left to go to their hotel. I told you, Ed, I didn't want them sniffing around, but Perry went ahead and called them in. Now I've got two feds thinking they can waltz in and handle things better than we can."

The Mayor let out a deep breath on the other end of the line. "Yeah, and I told you to do your job. Why the hell did Perry go behind your back?"

"Because he always has to do everything by the book," Becan growled. "Freakin' boy scout, that one. I'm telling you, these agents are gonna make a mess of this. And get this—one of them, Beretti? She thinks she's running the show." He paused, his lips curling into a sneer. "You should see her. Pretty blonde thing, walking in here like she owns the place. Bet she thinks her good looks will get her further than her badge. Probably why she's got this job in the first place."

The Mayor ignored the comment. "Clearly, your Chief Deputy doesn't respect you, Becan—and that's on you. Perry went behind your back because he didn't trust you to handle this."

Becan leaned back in the driver's seat, shaking his head. "Yeah, well, I don't have time to babysit a couple of outsiders while they try to take over. I'm telling you, Ed, this is a bad idea. We don't need feds. We need to handle this quietly, before they bring the media in. Last thing we need is some headline about our little town getting torn apart by wolves or whatever monster they think it is."

The Mayor's voice softened. "I'll see what I can do, Becan. Just keep them off the radar for now. We can't have the press sniffing around, especially with the election coming up."

"Damn right we can't," Becan muttered. "I'll do what I can, but Perry's making this harder than it needs to be."

After another exchange of grievances, Becan hung up and tossed the phone onto the passenger seat. He glanced into the rearview mirror, his face still twisted with frustration. Beretti and Jacobi were a problem he didn't need, but now they were here—and they weren't leaving without stirring up trouble.

He grunted, turning the key in the ignition. "Damn feds."

As he pulled out of the station lot, he continued to mutter to himself. He had no intention of letting those agents disrupt the order of things, especially when he had spent years making sure everything in his town ran smoothly—for himself, at least. And now, with Beretti's sharp eyes on him and her partner at her side, he felt the walls closing in.

But he wasn't about to let some out-of-towners, no matter how attractive or smart they thought they were, come in and turn his world upside down.

TWENTY-THREE

The hotel room was brightly lit, the soft hum of the overhead light filling the quiet space as Beretti and Jacobi sat across from each other. The small table between them was scattered with files, reports, and a large, unfolded map that Beretti had been poring over for the past half hour. Outside, the town bustled with a steady stream of traffic, but despite the clear day, an unease lingered—an unspoken awareness of the recent violence simmering beneath the surface.

Jacobi sat on the brink of the bed, the coroner's reports spread out in his lap. His expression tightened as he scanned the pages, gruesome details jumping out at him with each read. Across from him, Beretti leaned over the table, tracing her fingers along the map where the attacks had taken place.

"There's no clear pattern," she muttered, her eyes shifting between the red marks on the map. "Other than the attack on Les—where it likely followed him home—the campground and the sisters' house are in completely different parts of town. It just feels random."

Jacobi glanced up, his mind still on the autopsy reports. "Maybe it's just wandering and attacking whoever it comes across."

"Maybe," Beretti replied.

He flipped to another page in the report and grimaced at what he was reading. "The first attack, the camper... that poor guy didn't stand a chance. According to the coroner, he was torn apart—clawed, bitten, and fed on. But here's what sticks with me."

Beretti arched an eyebrow, looking up from the map. "What's that?"

Jacobi held up a page, pointing to the bite radius and the unusual teeth pattern. "The bite radius on this thing is nearly nine inches—double the size of any wolf you'd find around here. And look at this," he said, his finger tracing the marks. "It has extra teeth, serrated along the edges. It's like a wolf's bite but… wrong. More deadly, more efficient."

Beretti's expression hardened with grim recognition. "Well, that sounds exactly like a Dogman."

Jacobi nodded, flipping to another page, his expression darkening. "Then there are the sisters. One found inside the house, the other outside, behind a shed. Only the one by the shed had been fed upon. The coroner's report says the wounds were identical to the camper's—same claw marks, same massive bite radius."

Beretti leaned back in her chair, arms crossed as she processed the information. "And the one behind the shed… you think she was dragged out there, or was she attacked outside?"

"The report suggests she was trying to escape," Jacobi replied. "Maybe she was already injured and didn't make it far. Either way, the creature fed on her."

Beretti turned back to the map, her eyes scanning the locations. "And then there's Les Fay," Jacobi continued, pulling the latest report from the pile. "Last night's attack. According to what Perry told us, Les had just gotten home from the hunting trip when the creature attacked him."

Beretti frowned. "The sheriff organized that trip, didn't

he?"

"Yeah," Jacobi said, flipping through his notes. "He put the party together to track down this 'large wolf' that everyone's been talking about. Les and a few others had spent hours in the forest hunting it. But after they called it off, Les drove home—and that's when the supposed Dogman attacked."

Beretti stared at the map, her mind racing. "You think it followed him home?"

Jacobi leaned forward, considering her words. "It's possible. If they were close enough, if it saw them… it could have tracked him back to his house."

Beretti tapped her finger on the map, tracing a line between the hunting area and Les's home. "That would mean this thing is aware of them. It knows it's being hunted."

Jacobi nodded. "And it's not running. It's not afraid of humans at all."

The unsettling realization settled heavily in the room. Jacobi picked up the phone on the nightstand, glancing at Beretti. "We should check on Les, see if he's able to talk."

Beretti nodded as Jacobi dialed the hospital's number, waiting while it rang. After a moment, he began speaking to someone on the other end.

"Hi, this is Special Agent Noah Jacobi with the FBI. We need to know if Les Fay is able to speak," Jacobi said, keeping his voice calm but firm. "His wife, Laney Fay, is there with him?"

He paused as the nurse responded, his face relaxing slightly. "He's conscious and able to talk? That's great. We're on our way."

Jacobi hung up and turned to Beretti. "Les is stable, and his wife is with him. We should head over to the hospital."

Beretti stood, grabbing her jacket from the back of the chair. "Good. Let's go."

The two agents gathered their notes and headed out of the room. They were about to speak with a man who had come face-to-face with the Dogman—and lived to tell the tale.

But the question was: would it give them the answers they needed to stop the creature before it struck again?

TWENTY-FOUR

The hospital room was dim, the faint scent of antiseptic lingering in the air as Jacobi and Beretti entered, their footsteps muffled by the linoleum floor. Les Fay lay in the bed, his face pale and bruised, thick bandages covering his side and back where the creature had attacked him. His arm was secured in a sling, immobilizing his dislocated shoulder, with additional padding around the joint to keep it stable. His wife, Laney, sat beside him, her hands folded tightly in her lap, her face a mixture of exhaustion and fear. She glanced up as the agents approached, her eyes flickering with uncertainty.

"Mr. and Mrs. Fay," Jacobi greeted them softly, pulling up a chair beside the bed. "We're Special Agents Jacobi and Beretti with the FBI. We have to ask you some questions about the attack if that's ok?"

Les nodded weakly, his gaze shifting between the two agents. His voice was hoarse when he finally spoke. "I'll tell you what I can."

Beretti stood by the window, her arms crossed as she listened, her eyes never leaving Les. She could see the strain on his face, the deep lines etched into his skin from the trauma he had experienced.

Jacobi leaned forward slightly, his tone gentle but direct. "Les, can you walk us through what happened last night?"

Les took a deep breath, wincing as he adjusted himself in the bed. "It was about 1 a.m. when I finally got home. We'd been out hunting all night—me, Sheriff Becan, and a few other deputies and hunters. The sheriff had organized the trip to track down that big wolf everyone's been talking about."

He paused, frowning as if struggling to put his feelings into words. "I've been a hunter since I was a kid. Spent my whole life in the woods, and I've never been afraid of it. Not once." He glanced up, still shaken. "But then…then I saw that footprint on the trail. The one Chief Deputy Perry stopped to look at." He shook his head slowly, as if trying to make sense of it. "It was…huge. I mean, bigger than…than anything I've ever seen." He swallowed, his voice dropping. "That's when I knew something was wrong. The whole night felt off, like we were being watched. I was unusually jittery. Figured maybe I was tired, but that feeling wouldn't go away."

Beretti glanced at Jacobi, then back to Les. "And when you were driving home?"

Les nodded slowly. "Yeah. On the drive back, it got worse. That feeling of something being wrong, like something was waiting for me. I kept looking in the rearview mirror, half-expecting to see something following me, but there was nothing. Still, the feeling wouldn't go away. I just kept telling myself it was nerves after being in the forest all night."

He hesitated, his brow furrowing deeper. "But then I pulled into the driveway. That's when I saw it. It ran across the driveway—fast, too fast for me to get a good look. But it was on two legs, and it was hairy. I thought maybe it was just a trick of the light or a deformed bear at first, but… no, I knew. I knew something was wrong. I could feet it in my gut."

His voice wavered as he recalled the moment, his hands trembling slightly on the blanket. "I sat there in the car for a few minutes, trying to calm down, looking out every window. It was dead quiet. Not a single sound outside." He took a shaky breath, glancing over his shoulder as if he were back in that moment. "I kept telling myself to calm down and it was just my mind playing tricks on me. But my wife and boy were in the house, sleeping. I knew I had to get inside, to make sure they were safe." His grip tightened on an invisible shotgun as he spoke. "After a while, I grabbed my gun and opened the car door. I was hoping I had just worked myself up over nothing, but…"

Jacobi leaned in, nodding. "But?"

Les's face twisted with fear. "As soon as I stepped out and headed for the porch, it came out of nowhere—like a damn linebacker. Tackled me before I even knew what was happening. I didn't see it, didn't even hear it coming."

Laney's grip tightened on her lap as Les recounted the attack, her knuckles pale. Beretti noticed and glanced at her before turning back to Les.

Laney took a shaky breath, her voice barely holding steady as she spoke. "I'd fallen asleep on the couch, waiting for Les to get home. I woke up to this… scream. Just awful, primal. A sound I never want to hear again."

She swallowed hard, the memory clearly haunting her. "I didn't know what was happening—I just jumped up and ran to the door, flicked on the porch light." She closed her eyes, the horror flashing across her face. "And that's when I saw it...that thing, right there, tearing into him.

Jacobi turned his attention to her, his tone gentle. "What did you see, Mrs. Fay?"

Laney hesitated, her eyes dropping to the floor as if the memory was too much to bear. "It was... big. Tall. Covered in dark hair. And its face..." She shuddered, her voice trembling. "Its face was twisted, like something out of a nightmare. It had these glowing eyes... almost like it wasn't real. And the teeth..." Her voice dropped to a whisper. "It had too many teeth for its mouth, all crammed in there. Sharp, overlapping, like they didn't fit. When it looked up at me, it felt like it was staring right into my soul. It was the most horrible thing I've ever seen."

Beretti frowned, considering her words carefully. "Was it on all fours?"

Laney shook her head, her face paling at the memory. "No...no, it wasn't. It was hunched over Les on two feet, like it was...almost human." She swallowed hard, struggling to find the right words. "But everything about it was wrong."

Jacobi scribbled a note in his pad, then asked, "You said it took off after the light came on. Did you see where it went?"

Laney shook her head. "Just straight into the woods across from the house. One second it was on top of Les, and the next it was gone."

"Thank you, both of you," Jacobi said gently, closing his notepad. "I know this has been difficult for you both, but this information is crucial. It helps us understand what we're dealing with."

Les looked up, his voice strained. "What... what is it? Do you know?"

Beretti hesitated, glancing at Jacobi before answering. "We believe it's something... unique. Something very dangerous."

Les's eyes darkened, his hand trembling as he spoke. "It's not just a wolf, is it?"

"No," Jacobi replied, his voice low. "It's not."

Laney's looked up and met Beretti's gaze, her face pale as she struggled to find her words. "Have... have you seen one of these things before?"

Beretti paused, choosing her words carefully. "Not this

exact one, no. But its type? Yes."

Laney sat back, her eyes widening as she absorbed the implication—that there was more than one of these creatures in the world. She looked down, her fingers gripping the edge of the chair, then slowly glanced back up at Beretti, her expression softening with an unexpected resolve.

"I'll pray for the both of you," she whispered, her voice steady.

Beretti nodded, a flicker of gratitude in her eyes. "Thank you, Laney. We'll need it."

"We'll leave you two to rest," Jacobi said, turning back to the Fays. "But if you think of anything else, no matter how small, please let us know."

Laney nodded silently, her hand reaching for Les's as Jacobi and Beretti headed toward the door.

As they stepped into the hallway, Jacobi turned to Beretti. "There's no question about it—we're clearly dealing with a Dogman."

Beretti nodded, her eyes dark with concern. "If it's hunting this close to town, going after people right on their porches, it's just a matter of time before it attacks again."

Jacobi glanced down the corridor, his jaw set. "We know how dangerous these things get once they start feeling emboldened. Let's get something to eat and put together a plan ASAP."

Beretti's gaze sharpened. "Agreed. But first, I think we should take a look at the sisters' place. We might find something useful."

Jacobi nodded. "Good call. Let's get over there."

TWENTY-FIVE

Jacobi parked the SUV just outside the sisters' home, set along the edge of dense trees and overgrown brush. A light breeze rustled through, catching on the tattered strands of police tape, which flapped like streamers around the property, a grim reminder of the recent horror. Beretti stepped out first, her boots crunching on the gravel as she took in the scene. Now, standing on the same ground, the terror felt disturbingly close, an unwelcome guest lingering in the air.

They walked in silence toward the back of the house, Jacobi nodding toward the shed where Sofia had been found. Beretti's eyes lingered on the bloodstained ground near the shed, patches of earth marked with dark stains that resisted time and weather. She followed the faint tracks that seemed to lead into the edge of the forest.

"This is where they found Sofia," Jacobi said quietly, his eyes tracing the blood-streaked earth. "Dragged out here, torn apart, and discarded."

Beretti walked slowly toward the shed, feeling a chill as she neared its front. The door hung crookedly, shattered around the edges, splinters and shards of wood scattered on the ground. She paused, taking in the ominous stillness before looking inside.

The interior was dim, the faint scent of oil and metal still lingering, reminders of Sofia's work here. Beretti could almost picture her there, crouched over a project, her back to the doorway, oblivious to the danger creeping closer.

"She was a mechanic," Beretti murmured, almost to herself. "She probably came out here to work like any other night."

Jacobi moved beside her, his eyes scanning the broken doorframe and the dark space inside. "If she was focused on her work, she might never have heard it approach. Didn't even have a chance to defend herself."

Beretti nodded, gritting her teeth. "I bet they loved it here. The privacy, the quiet of it all... this place must have felt like freedom."

But that same privacy, the isolation that had once drawn them here, had left them exposed to the worst of horrors.

The flashlight in Beretti's hand revealed fragments of a lived-in life interrupted—a corner of a framed photo knocked askew, and bloody streaks all over the floor, as though something had stepped in a pool of blood by the back door and tracked it down the hallway. Dark smears stretched across the floorboards, adding to the haunting stillness of the scene.

They moved closer to Layla's bedroom, the narrow space leading them to a truly gruesome scene. Beretti pushed the door open, her flashlight cutting through the quietness of the room. Blood spattered across the walls, bedframe, and floor, each streak telling its own story of panic and terror.

"She never stood a chance," Jacobi murmured, his voice tight as he surveyed the damage. The claw marks gouged deep into the walls and bedframe were chilling, clear signs of the attacker's brute strength. "She fought back, but...this is beyond anything I've seen."

Beretti moved carefully around the room, studying the claw marks, the spattered blood. "This wasn't a wild animal attacking at random," she said, her tone clipped. "It was targeted. It came in for her. And then it went right back out through there," she added, gesturing to the back door.

They exchanged a look, a grim understanding passing between them: this killer was anything but ordinary. Jacobi snapped a few photos before they turned to leave.

Outside, Beretti lingered a moment, casting her gaze across the rugged landscape, the thick trees that bordered the sisters' home, the open fields beyond. She could understand why they had loved it here, and it struck her how this peaceful haven had turned into a place of unimaginable terror.

TWENTY-SIX

Stone's Grill had a cozy, worn-in feel, the kind of place where locals lingered and the scent of grilled meat hung thick in the air. Deputy Perry had recommended it, saying they'd serve up the best steaks in town—along with some privacy. Beretti and Jacobi sat in a corner booth, the clatter of plates and low hum of conversation filling the space around them. Outside, the sun was dipping low, casting deepening streaks of light through the large front windows.

Beretti leaned back in her seat, fingers tracing the edge of the menu as her thoughts flicked through every detail they had on the case. Across from her, Jacobi was scrolling intently on his phone through local social media groups, searching for any reports or rumors that might shed light on the creature's recent movements.

"People are starting to lose it," Jacobi muttered, his eyes fixed on the screen.

Beretti looked up, folding her arms. "What do you mean?"

Jacobi handed her the phone, the screen glowing with posts from the town's local Facebook group. "Look at this. Half the town is in a frenzy. There's constant chatter about these attacks—people arguing about what kind of animal it is, what the sheriff's doing—or not doing—and now, folks are starting to take matters into their own hands."

Beretti scrolled through the posts, her expression tightening. The town's residents were scared, and the fear was evident in the comments. People were speculating wildly—everything from wolves to mountain lions to something more sinister, something people didn't want to believe. But what troubled her more was the number of posts questioning Sheriff Becan's competence. People were accusing him of doing nothing, of covering up the truth. The growing distrust in the town's leadership was clear.

"Great," Beretti muttered. "This is exactly what we don't need. Fear breeds recklessness, and with the sheriff sitting on his hands, the townsfolk think they are on their own."

Jacobi nodded. "It gets worse. Look at this guy."

He pointed to a post by someone named Eunice Rogers. The man had posted in all caps, urging people to message him if they were interested in joining a night watch. His profile photo showed him standing with a pair of rifles, looking smug and ready for action. The post had dozens of comments, most in support of the idea, with people agreeing that something needed to be done. Others, however, voiced concerns about untrained, jittery locals wandering around with guns, hunting what they assumed was a large wolf.

"Night watch?" Beretti frowned, shaking her head. "This could get people killed. A bunch of scared men and women walking around with guns, thinking they're gonna find a wolf? They could end up shooting each other—or worse, provoking the Dogman."

Jacobi leaned back in the booth, rubbing his temple. "Yeah. People are getting desperate. They don't know what they're dealing with, and they're not going to wait for the sheriff to take action. Hell, some of them don't even believe it's a wolf anymore."

Beretti glanced at Jacobi. "And what do they think it is?"

Jacobi sighed, scrolling through the comments. "A lot of

people are saying it's a cryptid—Bigfoot, a werewolf, or maybe a rabid wolf gone rogue. Plenty of them are laughing it off, but you can sense the fear underneath. This town's scared enough to believe just about anything at this point."

Beretti nodded slowly, setting the phone down. "This isn't good. Panic like this? It's going to make our job a hell of a lot harder. If those folks on the night watch run into the Dogman, they'll be torn apart. And if they see us out there hunting, they might mistake us for the creature."

Jacobi chewed on that thought for a moment before speaking. "And the sheriff? He hasn't said a damn thing publicly. He's letting this stew."

Beretti sighed. "Of course he is. It's typical. He's probably hoping this will blow over, but with another attack, that's not going to happen. And now we've got this Rogers guy trying to rally a posse of untrained, armed civilians. They're scared, and they're going to do something stupid."

Their food arrived—Jacobi's steak with paired sides of mashed potatoes and sautéed vegetables, and Beretti's salmon served with seasoned greens. The feeling of hunger was gone, and now a growing unease was settling in their stomachs.

Beretti picked up her fork but didn't eat. "We need to get

ahead of this. The more time that passes without any official response, the more these people are going to feel like they have to act on their own. And when scared people act, they make mistakes. We can't let this town spiral out of control."

Jacobi scrolled through his phone, his face tightening. "Check this out. Some guy posted earlier that he saw a large animal running along a ridgeline. Thought it was just a wolf at first, but then he grabbed his binoculars to get a better look."

Beretti cocked an eyebrow. "And?"

Jacobi continued, "He says it stopped dead in its tracks, then stood up on two legs, looking around like it was scoping the area. Said it looked like a deformed hyena mixed with a shepherd—big, hunchbacked, with this mangy, twisted look to it."

Beretti's expression darkened. "Sounds like a Dogman."

Jacobi nodded, passing her the phone. "Yeah. Describes it standing there, scanning the horizon, like it knew he was watching. But of course, the comments are ripping him apart—calling him crazy, saying he's had too much to drink. The usual."

Beretti glanced over the man's post, taking in the vivid details of what he'd seen. She shook her head, passing the phone back. "They'd rather mock him than believe it's real. Easier to make a joke out of something terrifying than face it."

Beretti took a bite of her salmon, finally, and chewed thoughtfully. "We can't stop these folks from forming their little night watch, but we can try to mitigate the damage. Keep an eye on them, make sure they don't get themselves killed or get in our way when we start tracking this thing."

Jacobi nodded. "I've already got a list of people who've commented on that post. If we need to, we can reach out and see what their plans are—maybe talk some sense into a few of them."

Beretti gave him a sidelong glance. "That's a lot of work. You ready to spend your night talking people down from playing hero?"

Jacobi smirked. "Better than cleaning up after a bunch of trigger-happy guys shoot at anything that moves."

Beretti took another bite of her salmon. "Fine. We keep an eye on the night watch, but I want to be clear: if it looks like they're getting themselves in over their heads, we pull the plug. This town's on edge, and we don't need more dead bodies."

Jacobi nodded, picking up his fork. "Agreed. I'll keep monitoring the group and see if Eunice Rogers posts anything else."

As they neared the end of their meal, Beretti put her fork down and glanced at Jacobi. "We need a plan for tonight. We can't let these guys wander around unchecked."

Jacobi nodded. "What are you thinking?"

Beretti leaned forward, her voice low. "We'll drive around tonight, keep an eye out for the dogman—and the posse, too. Let's see if they're actually doing more than just talking big." She reached for her phone. "I'll loop Perry in, coordinate with his patrols. He needs to know what we're planning."

Jacobi grinned. "Sounds like a plan. I'll be ready."

They finished up, the last of their food growing cold on the plates, as the seriousness of the situation settled over them. Outside, the sun had fully set, and the town had slipped into an uneasy calm. The quiet streets betrayed the growing fear simmering just beneath the surface, the town's people waiting for the next attack—waiting for something to break.

As they left the steakhouse and stepped into the cool

night air, Beretti glanced at Jacobi. "I'll give ASIC Ward a call to update him before we head out."

"Sounds good," Jacobi replied as he headed to the SUV.

TWENTY-SEVEN

The night air was cool, and the streets were mostly deserted as Beretti and Jacobi pulled into the small parking lot just off Main Street. The only sound that could be heard for miles was the car engine, with the occasional rustle of leaves carried by the breeze. Parking their car, they waited while keeping an eye on the empty streets. Not much stirred in this quiet town, but Beretti could feel the anxiety hanging in the air, thick and oppressive.

A few minutes later, headlights appeared down the road, and Perry's patrol car came into view. He pulled in beside them, and the door creaked as he stepped out, adjusting his jacket against the evening chill. His face was worn, a clear indication of the toll the recent events had taken on him.

"Evening," Perry greeted them, his voice low but alert.

"Evening Perry," Jacobi nodded, stepping out of the car.

Beretti followed suit, closing her door softly as the three gathered near the front of the vehicles.

Perry leaned against his car, arms crossed. "What've you got for me?"

Jacobi handed over his phone, the screen glowing with the local social media posts he'd been monitoring all day. "The town's getting scared. People are forming their own night watch. A guy named Eunice Rogers is trying to rally a bunch of townsfolk to patrol the streets with rifles, thinking they're gonna take down a wolf."

Perry frowned as he scrolled through the posts. "Yeah, I know Rogers. One of those Sovereign Citizen types—probably has a huge stash of guns hidden away somewhere. He did ten years for manslaughter back in the early 2000s. He's had a string of petty crimes since, nothing too serious, but enough to show he's the kind of guy who doesn't play by the rules. Gets angry fast, too. If he's leading the charge on this, we're going to have trouble."

Beretti lifted one eyebrow. "And the sheriff still hasn't done anything about this?"

Perry shook his head. "No, I doubt he even has Facebook, let alone sees it as a way to stay informed. But like I said, Rogers is the last person you'd want leading a group of armed citizens through town. He's unpredictable, and the last thing we need is someone like him taking matters into his own hands."

Jacobi glanced at Beretti, his expression growing more serious. "Great. Just what we need—a heavily armed, easily angered ex-con with a posse of scared townsfolk."

"Exactly," Perry muttered. "And knowing Rogers, he's probably got enough firepower to take down an army. I've had run-ins with him before. He likes to push boundaries, and he's not going to back down if someone challenges him. This could get ugly fast."

Beretti sighed, handing the phone back to Jacobi. "We'll keep an eye on him. Hopefully, he's all talk, but we need to be prepared in case he's not."

Perry gave a curt nod. "Two of my deputies and I will be patrolling tonight. Normally, it'd just be two of us, but with everything going on, I figured an extra pair of eyes wouldn't hurt."

"And the sheriff okayed that?" Beretti asked.

Perry snorted, shaking his head. "I haven't seen the sheriff since he stormed out after you two left. Probably at home in his recliner with a beer. No, he didn't okay it. But I'm not waiting around for him to make a decision."

Beretti crossed her arms, exchanging a glance with Jacobi. "Where's the sheriff been all this time?"

Perry shifted his weight, frustration evident. "He's been scarce the past few days. The only reason he even put together that hunting party last night was because the Mayor—his brother-in-law—pushed him into it. Otherwise, he'd have done nothing, chalking it up to 'wildlife problems' the town has to deal with."

Jacobi frowned. "How does he get away with being so lazy?"

Perry gave a weary shrug. "'Cause he's got me, I guess. Me and the other deputies—we do the job, and he takes the credit."

"So, the Mayor had to get involved," Beretti said, frowning.

Perry nodded. "That's right. If it wasn't for family pressure, we'd still be waiting for him to do anything. We're dealing with a sheriff who's more concerned with keeping things quiet than actually solving the problem."

Beretti nodded grimly. "Got it."

Perry looked up at the quiet streets, his expression tense. "I've got to start my patrol. Two of my deputies will be covering the north and east parts of town. I'll head toward the west end, near Les' house, and circle back around. Hopefully, we'll cross paths with this night watch before they get too deep into trouble."

"We'll be driving around the outskirts, keeping an eye out as well," Beretti said. "I'll call you if we see anything."

Perry gave a curt nod and pushed off from his car, heading back to the driver's seat. Before he climbed in, he paused and glanced back at them. "Watch yourselves tonight. Rogers is the type of guy who thinks he knows better than anyone. If you cross him, he might not hesitate to pull the trigger."

"We'll keep that in mind," Jacobi replied. "We'll stay in touch."

With that, Perry climbed into his patrol car, the engine rumbling to life. He pulled out of the lot and disappeared down the street, his taillights fading into the darkness. Beretti watched him go, her mind already racing through possibilities. Rogers was a loose cannon, and the sheriff's absence wasn't helping.

Before they got back into their car, Jacobi turned to Beretti. "Let's check the armory. We need to be prepared for any situation we might encounter tonight."

Beretti nodded. "Agreed. If this Dogman crosses our path, or if we run into Rogers and his posse, I don't want us under-prepared."

Jacobi popped the trunk, and the glow of the trunk light revealed a solid array of weapons, all neatly organized and ready for use. The first thing Jacobi pulled out was a .308 Winchester bolt-action rifle, sleek and powerful. "This should be enough to punch through any tough hide we come across."

Beretti reached for the .300 Win Mag with a synthetic stock. The heft of it felt good in her hands, and she gave it an approving nod. "This'll put something down for sure." She checked the scope and the ammunition, nodding in satisfaction. High-caliber rifles were necessary for dealing with cryptids—something that might shrug off anything less.

Jacobi loaded a magazine into the AR-10 they had in the back, its 7.62x51mm rounds packing serious stopping power. "We've got the firepower to handle anything—whether it's a cryptid or a bunch of jittery folks with rifles. Let's hope we don't have to use it."

Beretti checked the ammunition belts, double-checking each weapon before securing most of them back in the trunk and keeping two out for easy access. "All high-caliber and ready for a fight," she said. "If it comes to that."

Jacobi closed the trunk, and they both stood by the car for a moment, the gravity of what lay ahead settling heavily in the quiet space between them.

"You think the sheriff's hiding something? Or is he just plain lazy?" Jacobi asked, in a quiet tone.

Beretti shrugged, her eyes scanning the darkened streets. "Could be both. But whatever his deal is, it doesn't change the fact that this town's a powder keg waiting to go off. We need to be ready for whatever happens tonight."

Jacobi nodded, taking in the gravity of her words. "Let's hope this 'posse' doesn't make things worse."

They climbed back into the car, Jacobi turning the key and bringing the engine to life. The soft hum filled the quiet night, and they drove toward the outskirts of town, where the darkness deepened, and the sense of danger grew more intense. Beretti kept her eyes on the tree line, looking for anything that moved.

As they drove, Jacobi broke the silence. "So, we're keeping

tabs on the night watch, and the Dogman. Anything else?"

Beretti chuckled and glanced over. "I think that's enough to deal with."

Jacobi nodded, smiling to himself. The night was just beginning, and it was already clear—it was going to be a long one.

TWENTY-EIGHT

irk Sandoval slouched deeper into the worn-out cushions of his couch, a half-drunk beer nestled in his grip, the flickering TV casting a dull light across the dingy trailer. *Duck Dynasty* was playing, and he snorted at something Uncle Si had said about "hunting being a man's calling." Tammy was banging around in the kitchen, microwaving whatever frozen garbage she called dinner. The dogs outside had been barking for what felt like hours, their frenzied yelps cutting through the usual silence. His four Rottweilers were always loud, but tonight their barking was different—shrill, wild, almost like they were spooked by something lurking in the dark.

"Shut those damn mutts up!" Dirk barked, slamming his

beer down on the coffee table hard enough to rattle the empty cans.

Tammy yelled back, "I'm making dinner! You go shut them up!"

Dirk sneered, rolling his eyes. "You call putting pizza pockets in the microwave dinner? I call it lazy."

"Shut the hell up!" she snapped, her voice sharp but indifferent, knowing full well that he wasn't about to do anything except complain.

The barking grew louder, more frantic. Dirk's patience snapped. He shoved himself off the couch, standing a little too fast as the room spun slightly from the beers he'd downed over the past few hours. "Christ," he muttered, rubbing his hand across his stubbled jaw. "You're lucky I'm even getting up, Tam."

"Yeah, you're a real hero," Tammy shot back, not bothering to look at him as the microwave beeped behind her.

Dirk grabbed the .22 rifle leaning near the front door, the one he kept around more for show than anything else. "These damn dogs," he grumbled as he swung open the door and stomped out onto the porch, rifle in hand.

Dirk swaggered out onto the porch, his boots clunking against the wooden boards, the cold night air smacking him in the face. His arrogant attitude never faltered—he was Dirk Sandoval, after all. No one scared him. But tonight? Something felt off. The barking, which had been so loud moments ago, suddenly stopped dead the second he stepped outside.

"The hell?" he muttered, his brow furrowing in drunken confusion. The night was strangely still, quieter than it had any right to be. He squinted toward the wire cage where his Rottweilers were kept, their silhouettes barely visible in the faint moonlight. All four dogs were huddled in their houses, not a single one growling or barking. They looked... scared. And that wasn't normal.

Dirk scoffed. "You damn mutts scared of a little breeze?" He stomped down the creaky steps and made his way toward the cage. His boots scraped over the packed dirt, each step slower than the last as a prickle of unease settled in his gut. Not that he'd ever admit it. Dirk Sandoval wasn't scared of anything—or so he liked to tell himself.

"Hey! Get out here!" he barked at the dogs, rattling the cage with his rifle. But they stayed hidden, their eyes peeking out, wide with fear. Dirk frowned. These weren't timid dogs. They were trained to attack, and yet they were cowering like frightened puppies.

He squatted down by the cage, banging on it again. "What the hell's wrong with you?"

Suddenly, a new sound broke through the silence—a series of quick, heavy footsteps thudding around one of the junk cars that littered his property. Dirk's head jerked up, his eyes narrowing. "Who the hell's out there?" he shouted, his tone dripping with irritation more than concern. He'd never been one to think before acting, especially after a few drinks.

No answer. Just the quiet night, a little too quiet for his liking.

Dirk stood up, his grip tightening on the rifle. "I swear to God, if you're messing around on my property, I'll blow your goddamn head off!" He stomped forward, puffing out his chest on his 6ft 4 pot-bellied frame.

As he rounded the rusted hulk of an old sedan, his breath fogged up in the cold air, and his heart started to pound faster. The rustling noise grew louder. "Who's there?" he yelled, taking another step forward, rifle raised. He wasn't scared, just pissed off. Dirk Sandoval didn't back down—he was too stubborn, too arrogant to realize when he should.

A sudden movement in the corner of his eye made him

whip his head to the side. His heart leapt, but he covered it up with a snarl, raising his rifle. "I said, show yourself!"

Nothing. The yard stretched out in front of him, a dark mess of broken-down cars and rusting metal parts. But the sound came again, a little further away this time, something heavy moving through the debris.

Dirk should've turned back. Any sane man would've. But not Dirk. His arrogance was too strong, even as a cold sweat broke out on his forehead. "Think you can mess with me? You got another thing coming," he muttered under his breath, taking another few steps toward the noise.

And then, from nowhere, a massive shape leaped onto the hood of one of the rusted-out cars in front of him. The impact was so heavy it made the metal groan under its weight. Dirk froze, his eyes wide as he took in the creature standing just a few feet away.

It was huge. Standing on four legs like some kind of nightmare version of a wolf, its fur dark and patchy. Its eyes, glowing in the faint moonlight, locked onto Dirk with a look that made his skin crawl. Its lips pulled back into a snarl, revealing jagged teeth, and a deep, guttural growl rumbled from its chest.

"What the fuck…" Dirk whispered, his hands trembling as he fumbled with the rifle. He took a shaky step back, nearly tripping over his own feet. His mouth was dry, his bravado gone.

The creature crouched low, muscles coiling as if ready to pounce.

Dirk's survival instincts finally kicked in, and he lifted the rifle, aiming at the creature's chest. But before he could steady his hands, its glowing eyes flicked to the weapon—and in an instant, it sprang off the car, disappearing into the darkness with terrifying speed.

He stood there, rifle still raised, aiming at nothing. As his breath came in quick, erratic bursts, he felt a sudden, shameful dampness and realized he'd wet himself. The intensity of what he'd witnessed pressed down on him, leaving him paralyzed in the silence.

For the first time in his life, Dirk Sandoval was genuinely scared. His hands shook as he slowly lowered the rifle. This wasn't some prank or a wild animal. It was something far worse, something he couldn't explain.

His legs felt weak, his bravado completely shattered as he stumbled back toward the trailer, keeping his eyes on the woods the whole time. He practically kicked the door open as he burst inside, slamming it shut behind him, his breath heavy and uneven. He was drenched in cold sweat, his face drained of color as he leaned against the door, his hands still shaking.

Tammy turned from the kitchen, munching on a pizza pocket. "What the hell's wrong with you?"

Dirk didn't answer. He just stood there, completely zoned out, in a daze.

"Dirk?"

He opened his mouth, but the words caught in his throat.

What the hell was that?

"You look like you've seen a ghost," Tammy said, stepping closer, her voice losing some of its usual bite.

Dirk finally looked up and met her gaze. "It wasn't no ghost."

"What, then?"

His eyes flicked toward the window, to the darkness outside. "It was a goddamn abomination."

TWENTY-NINE

Jacobi cracked open a can of Red Bull, the soft fizz breaking the quiet in the SUV. He took a long sip, the caffeine boost settling him as he kept one hand steady on the wheel. They'd swung by a gas station while on patrol, grabbing a few supplies to keep them going through the long night ahead.

Beside him, Beretti adjusted the spotlight controls, her eyes focused on the tree line as she directed the beam back and forth. Shadows danced along the road as the light sliced through the dark, each sweep illuminating only patches of dense forest before slipping back into black. The town felt charged with unease tonight, as if something was watching, just beyond their sight, ready to pounce at the perfect moment.

"You think it will show itself tonight?" Jacobi asked, breaking the silence, his hands steady on the wheel as he navigated the winding road.

Beretti shrugged, adjusting the spotlight. "Hard to say. Attacking humans is a huge risk—normally, they stay far away from us. But this one..." She trailed off, frowning. "It's desperate. I don't know what's driving it, but something must've changed to make it start going after people." She glanced out into the darkness. "Desperate animals take chances, and eventually, they slip up. I have a feeling we'll find it. Just a matter of time."

Jacobi chuckled softly. "You always have a feeling."

"Call it instinct," she replied with a smirk.

The spotlight beam drifted over the darkened woods, illuminating gaps between the trees with an unsettling clarity. Branches and trunks appeared briefly in the stark light, giving the forest an almost haunted quality before the scene was swallowed back into darkness. They were both on edge, but the quiet moments like this gave them room to talk, to lighten the mood.

"So... Noah Jacobi," Beretti said, glancing sideways at him. "Were your parents religious?"

Jacobi chuckled, a low, brief sound, like he'd heard the question a hundred times before. "Oh, yeah. Very religious. Old-school Catholic. I'm honestly surprised they didn't name me Moses or something even more biblical."

Beretti grinned. "Noah's pretty biblical. Are you close with them?"

Jacobi shook his head. "Haven't been for almost ten years. My decision to join the Marines didn't exactly go over well. They had...different plans for my life. Seminary school, maybe a nice, quiet life behind a pulpit."

Beretti raised an eyebrow, the spotlight casting a sharp beam of light through the trees. "Seminary? Doesn't seem like your style."

"Nope," Jacobi agreed. "That's part of the reason I haven't talked to them. They didn't approve of the Marines, didn't approve of much I did, really. It was easier to just... walk away."

"Must've been hard," Beretti said, her voice a little softer.

Jacobi shrugged. "It was. But you gotta live your life, right? Can't live someone else's dream forever."

Beretti nodded in agreement. "Amen to that."

Jacobi looked over at her, his curiosity piqued. "What about you, Beretti? Are your parents still around?"

A shadow crossed her face. "No. They died in a car crash when I was a teenager."

He paused, absorbing her words. "I'm really sorry to hear that." After a beat, he asked, "Are you close with any other family? Siblings?"

"No siblings," she replied. "But I am close with my uncle. He took me in after my parents passed. Raised me, really."

Jacobi took that in, a hint of admiration in his gaze. Then, something seemed to click. "Beretti... that's Italian, right?"

She nodded. "Yeah, Italian on my father's side. My mom's side is a little more complicated. My maternal grandmother was Karuk, and my grandfather was Swiss. Pretty mixed bag, actually."

Jacobi's eyes widened a little. "Oh, so you've got Native American heritage, too?"

Beretti nodded, a touch of pride in her voice. "Yep, I sure do."

Jacobi smiled, taking that in. "And I'm guessing the Swiss

side is where you got the blonde hair?"

"More than likely," she replied, her eyes glinting with a bit of humor.

Before he could ask her more, Beretti's phone buzzed in her lap. Perry's name flashed on the screen. She glanced at Jacobi, then answered, putting it on speaker.

"Perry?" she said, her voice suddenly more serious.

"Beretti, I'm out at the Sandoval property on McCallisters Lane," Perry's voice came through, tense and low. "Dirk Sandoval claims he saw something tonight. Says it was a giant hyena with amber eyes, at least 9 feet tall with hands instead of claws."

Beretti exchanged a glance with Jacobi, the two of them silently processing the description. "Go on," she said, keeping her voice steady.

"Sandoval's not the type to spook easily," Perry said, his voice lowering. "And he's the last guy who'd call law enforcement onto his property unless something was seriously wrong. But whatever he saw tonight has him rattled. His dogs went from barking like crazy to dead silent in seconds." Perry paused, meeting their eyes. "He said it just stood there, staring him down—and only bolted once he raised his rifle."

Jacobi tightened his grip on the steering wheel. "That fits with what we've been hearing."

Beretti nodded. "Where's his place?"

Perry gave her the location. "It's about two miles east of town. Place is littered with junk—old cars, parts everywhere. It's isolated enough that something could be lurking out here without anyone noticing."

"We'll do a sweep of the area," Beretti said, leaning back in her seat. "Then we'll head back into town, keep an eye on things."

"Good. I'm staying here a bit longer to see if it shows itself again."

Perry's tone grew a little more serious. "Stay sharp."

"We'll be ready," Beretti said, hanging up the phone.

Jacobi glanced over as Beretti punched "McCallister's Lane" into the GPS. They cruised a few more yards down the empty road before he muttered, "Guess it got desperate again tonight."

He guided the SUV into a U-turn, the tires crunching

softly on the dirt as they headed toward Sandoval's property.

Beretti nodded in agreement. "Yeah, but it's staying on the outskirts of town. And if it took off the moment Sandoval raised his rifle, it clearly knows what a gun can do." She paused, her eyes narrowing. "It's not just hunting—it's testing boundaries."

As they drove, Beretti turned the spotlight back on, sweeping the woods again. The air seemed heavier as they got closer to McDermott's isolated junkyard. She rested her hand near her sidearm, ready for whatever came next.

Jacobi slowed the car slightly as the dense forest loomed closer. "Hyena or not, this thing's out hunting."

"And we're going to find it," Beretti said firmly.

The road stretched out before them, long and foreboding, as they headed toward the unknown.

THIRTY

Angela Schwartz tapped the screen on her phone, confirming the pick-up from the local Thai restaurant. She let out a small sigh of relief. This was her last delivery of the night, and it was already approaching 9 p.m. She'd been on the go for almost four hours straight, darting around town, navigating quiet streets. Being one of only four Uber Eats drivers in town kept her busy, especially in the evenings when late-night orders came through.

She glanced at the order details: the Parkinsons, a house in a new subdivision on the edge of town. The area was typical for her deliveries—quiet, with newly built homes and neatly lined streets. Angela didn't think much of it. It was a normal delivery, just another stop before she could finally call it a night.

She parked by the curb, leaving the engine running, and grabbed the warm brown paper bag, the smell of food making her stomach growl—she hadn't eaten a thing since morning. Stepping out, she headed up the Parkinsons' smooth cement driveway, identical to the rest in the tidy subdivision. As she walked, she muttered to herself, "I'm so damn hungry. Nearly done."

As she was walking up the driveway, her footsteps tapping softly on the concrete, she heard a faint noise. Movement coming from the bushes near the neighbor's property. Angela paused, her heart giving a tiny jolt. She turned her head, eyes scanning the dark space between the houses, but nothing moved.

"Damn racoons always scare the crap outta me," she muttered to herself, forcing a small chuckle. The woods were nearby, so it made sense for animals to wander close.

Angela picked up her pace, walking a little faster as she neared the Parkinsons' front door. The house was brightly lit, the porch light casting a soft glow over the entryway. Right before she knocked, she saw a quick movement out of the corner of her eye. A blur—something fast, too fast to process.

Before Angela could react, something slammed into her. A strong, vice-like grip wrapped around her midsection, pulling her off her feet. Her scream caught in her throat as the creature dragged her toward the nearby bushes with terrifying speed. She thrashed, her legs kicking in the air, but the creature was too powerful, its fur rough and coarse against her skin.

The last thing Angela saw was the Parkinsons' porch light flickering in the distance as she was pulled into the darkness.

A moment later, Mr. Parkinson opened the front door, his brow wrinkled in mild annoyance. He expected to see the Uber Eats driver standing there with their food, but the porch was empty. His eyes dropped to the ground, where he spotted the brown paper bag lying near the steps.

"You can't even knock and leave it on the porch?" he muttered, stepping outside to grab the food. As he bent down, he heard the low hum of a car idling nearby.

Mr. Parkinson straightened up, looking toward the street. The Uber Eats driver's car was still running, parked awkwardly by the curb with no-one in it. A strange feeling crept into his stomach. He called out, his voice echoing through the quiet night.

"Hello? You out there?"

Nothing.

Mr. Parkinson glanced around, scanning the driveway and the road beyond. The car's headlights illuminated the empty street, but there was no sign of the driver. His unease grew stronger. Grabbing the bag of food, he hurried back inside, shutting the door behind him.

"Something's not right," he muttered, a chill crawling up his spine as he moved toward the living room. His hand instinctively went to his phone. He tapped the screen, checking for any recent notifications, then remembered—the doorbell camera.

He quickly opened the app on his phone and navigated to the doorbell camera feed, scrolling back to see what had happened. His wife's voice called out from the kitchen, a bit impatient.

"Where's our food?"

"Just a minute," Mr. Parkinson replied absently, his attention fully on the phone.

As the footage played, his heart pounded harder. The video showed the Uber Eats driver, a young woman, walking up the driveway with the bag of food in her hand, looking completely ordinary. She paused, glancing nervously toward the bushes, as though she'd heard something. After a moment's hesitation, she resumed walking. Then, out of nowhere, a dark blur shot into the frame—large, fast, and menacing.

And then she was gone.

Mr. Parkinson gasped, nearly dropping the phone. He stared in disbelief as he replayed the video. A massive creature had snatched the Uber driver right off his doorstep and dragged her into the bushes. His heart pounded, and he muttered, "Is that a fucking werewolf?" before stumbling back, whispering, "Holy shit…holy shit," over and over as he fumbled to dial 911.

The operator answered quickly, but his voice was shaking as he tried to explain what he had just witnessed.

"There's been… an attack. The Uber driver—she's was attacked. Something took her. I saw it on my camera—it dragged her away!"

The operator's voice was calm but urgent, asking for details. "Sir, can you explain what you saw? What took her?"

Mr. Parkinson was nearly breathless. "It was…huge! It

looked like a freaking werewolf! I know that sounds insane, but I have it on video. It came out of nowhere. Please, you must send someone! That poor, poor girl."

The operator assured him that help was on the way, but Mr. Parkinson's mind was reeling. His eyes dropped to the phone screen, where the image of the beast mid-attack was frozen in place. It was right there on his driveway, brutal and undeniable. It didn't seem real. But it was.

For a long moment, he stared toward the front door, dread settling over him. Swallowing hard, he turned and walked briskly to his office. He unlocked the safe, pulling out his gun with a shaky hand. He was freaking out thinking, "What if it comes back?" What if it wasn't finished yet? His eyes drifted toward the living room where his family were, and a wave of nausea swept over him.

THIRTY-ONE

The Dogman dragged Angela through the woods, her vision blurring as her body trembled with terror. Its grip around her midsection was like a vise, squeezing her ribs as it hurtled through the trees at terrifying speed. Sharp branches and jagged rocks tore into her skin, leaving raw scrapes and deep cuts along her arms, legs, and face. Pain seared through her, but the pressure on her chest was so intense it choked off any chance to scream. Her legs kicked feebly, her arms thrashing in desperation, but it was no use.

She couldn't make sense of what was happening—everything was moving too fast. *Does a bear have me?* She felt overwhelmingly petrified, her mind in a panic.

Then, abruptly, the creature stopped and dropped her to the ground. Angela's body sagged, hitting the cold earth as her head spun, each shallow breath a sharp stab of pain. Dazed, she looked up, finally able to take in the thing that had attacked her. The Dogman loomed over her, its hulking, fur-covered form silhouetted against the dark woods, with eyes that glowed a feral amber and teeth bared in a twisted snarl.

She didn't even have time to scream before it bent low, hot breath searing her skin. A sudden, piercing pain shot through her as its teeth sank deep into her neck, silencing her in an instant.

The world dimmed, her vision blurring at the edges, until everything slipped into blackness.

THIRTY-TWO

The tires screeched as Jacobi whipped the SUV around a corner, heading straight for the Parkinsons' subdivision. Beretti was in the passenger seat, clutching her phone tightly, listening to Perry on speaker. The report was bleak. Another attack.

"We're two minutes out," Jacobi said, his eyes fixed on the dark road ahead.

"Copy that," Perry's voice crackled over the line. "I'm already here, and we've got deputies securing the perimeter. But the thing took off toward the woods at the end of the street."

Beretti glanced at Jacobi, noting the hard set of his jaw.

"We're going in armed," she replied to Perry.

"Understood," Perry answered.

As they pulled into the subdivision, Jacobi killed the headlights, casting them into darkness. The Parkinsons' house loomed ahead—bright porch lights illuminating a tense scene. Deputy cruisers were parked haphazardly, deputies putting up tape to preserve the crime scene.

Perry was on the porch, speaking with Deputy Delvaney. His face was bleak as he spotted Beretti and Jacobi approaching. "A young Uber driver was attacked and dragged off into the woods," Perry said. "The homeowner has one of those doorbell cameras."

Jacobi turned to Mr. Parkinson. "Can you AirDrop me the footage please?"

Parkinson nodded, his hands trembling as he sent the video. "It happened so fast... one second she was walking up to the door, and the next..." He trailed off, swallowing hard. "I—I feel awful, like I should have done something. I'm still trying to wrap my head around it."

Jacobi glanced at the footage as it arrived, his eyes narrowing as he analyzed the scene. Then, he passed the phone to Beretti. The blurry figure of Angela being grabbed and dragged into the bushes by something large and fast sent a chill through the air.

Without missing a beat, Jacobi was already heading toward the SUV. "We're going after it."

Beretti shot him a look. "Slow down, Jacobi. We need to be careful." Her tone hinted at familiarity—she knew Jacobi liked to take charge and sometimes rushed into things.

He gave a quick nod, acknowledging her caution, but his pace remained quick. They grabbed their rifles from the back of the SUV and started prepping. Perry approached, flashlight and weapon at the ready.

"I'll join you," Perry said, stepping beside them. "Let's move."

Perry quickly called over to one of the deputies, giving instructions to hold the perimeter. "Stay sharp. We're going into the woods. Keep your eyes open and have Mr Parkinson write a statement."

The three of them walked down the road and moved toward the tree line. Jacobi, despite Beretti's warning, instinctively took the lead, moving swiftly. The lights of the subdivision faded behind them as they entered the dark woods, where the atmosphere immediately shifted. The air was heavy with the scent of damp earth and pine, and the temperature dropped.

With her usual methodical approach, Beretti bent down low, carefully inspecting the ground for any signs of tracks. She was careful, deliberate in her movements, while Jacobi pushed ahead, eager to close the distance.

"Jacobi," Beretti called softly, her voice cutting through the quiet. "Hold up."

Jacobi stopped, glancing back at her. He exhaled, realizing he had been moving too fast. He nodded, allowing her to catch up, but his impatience was clear.

After a few moments, Beretti found what she was looking for. She crouched, tracing a set of drag marks leading into a narrow trail. "This way," she whispered, motioning Jacobi and Perry closer.

They followed the narrow path deeper into the woods, each step calculated and quiet. No one spoke. Their flashlights tore through the darkness, but the silence was unnerving. Not a single insect or nocturnal creature stirred. It was as if the woods themselves had gone still in horror, unwilling to disturb the aftermath of what they'd seen.

Jacobi, his instincts sharp, scanned ahead, his rifle ready.

Beretti, behind him, kept her eyes on the ground, her senses heightened. Perry, bringing up the rear, was tense, every nerve on edge.

Then came a noise. A brief rustle, something heavy darting through the brush ahead of them—fast. Too fast to see.

Jacobi raised his hand to signal the others, stopping in his tracks. "Something's out there," he muttered, his grip tightening on his rifle.

Beretti's eyes narrowed. "Stay low," she whispered. "It's close."

They continued forward cautiously, the pressure rising with each step. Beretti's flashlight swept across the ground, picking up signs of movement—disturbed leaves, broken branches. Something had passed through recently.

The deeper they went, the denser the trees became, blocking out what little moonlight remained. The oppressive silence of the woods weighed heavily on them. And then, they smelled it.

"Blood," Beretti muttered under her breath, her stomach twisting.

Jacobi slowed his pace at last, his face hardening. "We're close."

The game trail opened up into a small clearing, and that's when they saw her.

Angela's body lay on the forest floor, mutilated and barely recognizable. Blood pooled around her, soaking the ground. The marks on her body were unmistakable—deep gashes, bite marks too large to belong to any ordinary predator.

Perry sucked in a breath, stepping back in horror. "Jesus…"

Beretti knelt down beside the body, her expression hardening as she examined the scene. "Nearly took her head off."

Jacobi's jaw tightened. "Damn it."

Perry's face was pale, his voice unsteady as he reached for his radio. Just as he fumbled with the device, a low, unsettling howl echoed from somewhere deep in the woods. The sound sent a chill through the group, each of them pausing to listen, the haunting call lingering in the air.

Swallowing hard, Perry finally pressed the button. "Dispatch, this is Chief Deputy Perry. We've found the body in the woods... his voice composed. We'll secure the scene for the Coroner. Over."

The radio crackled back, confirming the message. Perry looked at Beretti and Jacobi, his face tight with worry. "I'm going to need answers, and fast."

THIRTY-THREE

The morning sun filtered through the windows of the small café, casting a soft glow over the worn wooden tables and mismatched chairs. Beretti sat slouched in her seat, her eyes heavy with exhaustion. Across from her, Jacobi stirred his coffee absentmindedly, the events of the long night still playing on his mind. They had spent most of the night and early morning at the Parkinsons' house and exploring the woods, and now, they were trying to regroup over breakfast before heading back to their hotel for some much-needed rest.

Perry joined them, sliding into the booth with a tired sigh. He'd been quiet most of the night, processing what they had uncovered, but now that they were away from the scene, curiosity was getting to him.

After a tense silence, Perry leaned forward, glancing at Beretti. "All right, what exactly is that thing I saw on the video? What are we actually dealing with here? And don't sugarcoat it."

Beretti exchanged a quick glance with Jacobi before answering. "Dogman. It's a cryptid—a creature that's been reported in various places, mainly in North America. Think of it like a cross between a wolf and a man, but larger, stronger, and far more dangerous."

Perry sat there, absorbing her words, his face pale. After a long moment, he shook his head slowly. "So...you guys have known about these things?" He paused, and before she could answer, he muttered, "Of course you do. You hunt them, don't you?"

Beretti nodded. "Yes, we do. This isn't our first time dealing with a Dogman. I just came from Missouri, where two of them were terrorizing a small town."

Perry tightly clenched his jaw as he processed what she said. He had known, after last night's discovery, that they were dealing with something truly out of the ordinary, but hearing it laid out so plainly made it all too real. He leaned back in his chair, his eyes fixed on the table, trying to process it.

Perry chuckled nervously while shaking his head. "Well, hell… next thing you'll tell me you hunt Bigfoot too."

Beretti and Jacobi exchanged another glance, both of their faces dead serious.

Perry's laughter died in his throat as he looked at their expressions. "You gotta be kidding me," he said, his voice low and incredulous.

"Nope," Jacobi replied, sipping his coffee.

Perry stared at them for a moment, his mind racing. "So… what? Bigfoot, Dogman, all these things are real? Running around out there?"

Beretti shrugged. "Not everywhere, but they exist in certain places. The cases we handle tend to involve cryptids that cross paths with humans. Unfortunately, when that happens, things tend to get messy."

With fatigue sinking deeper into his bones, Perry wearily brushed his hand over his face. "I had a feeling right from the start that we were dealing with something extraordinary, but it's still tough to come to terms with."

The conversation lulled as the waitress brought over their food—plates of eggs, toast, and bacon for Jacobi and Perry, and a steaming bowl of oatmeal with a side of rye toast for Beretti. Quietly, they dined, trying to recover from the events of the night.

As they lingered over their meal, Jacobi looked up from his coffee, eyeing Perry with interest. "Hey, Perry, what's your story man? Did you grow up here?"

Perry nodded, a small smile crossing his face as he stirred his coffee. "Yep, born and raised in Enrick. Never really saw a reason to leave, you know? This town's in my blood."

Jacobi leaned in, genuinely curious. "So why haven't you gone for sheriff? You seem to be the one actually holding this place together."

Perry chuckled, a hint of self-deprecation in his tone. "Oh, I've thought about it once or twice. But politics…" He shook his head. "Not really my style. And the sheriff's position around here? It's as much about knowing the right people as it is about keeping folks safe. Becan's good at working the angles with the town's higher-ups. Me? I'm better suited to being out there, boots on the ground."

Beretti nodded, glancing at Jacobi. "Seems like you're

doing most of the heavy lifting here."

Perry shrugged, a slight grin playing on his face. "Maybe. But I don't mind. Like I said, this town's in my blood. Besides, someone's gotta be the one folks trust, the one who actually shows up when things go wrong."

Jacobi chuckled, lifting his coffee mug. "Well, here's to the real sheriff of Enrick."

As they finished their meal, Beretti set her spoon down and looked at Perry. "We're going to head back to the hotel, get some shut-eye. After we rest, we'll discuss with our superior what action we should take. We'll call you later this afternoon to update you."

Perry nodded, still a bit dazed from their conversation. "Yeah, alright. I'll get some shuteye too." He hesitated, then added, "Actually, this afternoon I need to head out to Norris Creek—might be worth your while to join me. Two local men, Tucker Leney and Bo Reyes have been missing over a week, and one of them left a note with just one word: *Norris.* At first I wondered if it was someone's name but when I googled it, I found a small dried up creek about eight miles out of town by that name. It's a long shot, but they could've headed out there...and maybe ran into the same thing we're dealing with."

Jacobi leaned forward. "You think they got themselves into trouble with the Dogman?"

Perry shrugged, a hint of frustration in his eyes. "Could be. From what I've heard, these two had made some decent money the past couple of months and no one knows what from or from where. Friends say Tucker was spooked though and they might have gotten in over their heads with something. Figured it wouldn't hurt to take a look."

Beretti exchanged a glance with Jacobi. "Alright, Perry. Ok if you meet us at the hotel this afternoon?"

Perry nodded, his expression resolute. "Yeah, I'll be there," he agreed.

They stood up, leaving money on the table to cover the bill and tip, and stepped outside into the bright morning light. Perry gave them a tired wave before heading toward his patrol car, his mind still spinning with the revelations from breakfast.

Beretti and Jacobi exchanged a glance as they watched him leave. "Think he's going to be alright?" Jacobi asked.

Beretti shrugged. "He'll have to be."

They climbed into their SUV, ready to head back to the

hotel for a few hours of much-needed sleep.

As Jacobi settled into the passenger seat, he stared out the window, watching the road where Perry's patrol car had disappeared. "I remember when I first found out Sasquatch and Dogmen were real—it took a week or more to even start accepting it," he said quietly. "Shook me up bad. But eventually…I had to accept there are things out there we don't fully understand."

Beretti nodded, starting the engine. "Yeah…it shatters everything you thought you knew about the world, about what we're told is real. Monsters don't exist, right?"

Jacobi gave a humorless chuckle. "I wish."

THIRTY-FOUR

The Mayor's office, usually a quiet hub of small-town politics, had turned into a boiling pot of frustration and fear. Outside, the crowd had swelled in number, voices raised in anger and panic. People were shoving, yelling at the closed doors of the office, demanding that the Mayor come out and do something about the creature terrorizing the town.

"We've had enough of this!" a man in a flannel shirt shouted, banging on the locked door. "What's the Mayor doing about these attacks? People are dying!"

A woman, clutching her child tightly, added her voice to the chaos. "How are we supposed to sleep at night? Do something before it's too late you morons!"

The receptionist inside the office was shaking, her eyes wide with fear as she glanced out the window. The crowd was growing more aggressive by the minute, and it felt like any second they might break down the door. She picked up the phone with trembling fingers and dialed Sheriff Becan's number. "Sheriff, you need to get over here now. It's getting out of control."

Sheriff Becan, sitting at his desk with his feet up, let out an annoyed sigh. "On my way," he muttered, hanging up the phone. He turned to the young deputy across from him. "Grab your cuffs. Looks like we've got some hotheads to deal with."

As they sped toward the Mayor's office, Becan caught a glimpse of himself in the rearview mirror. His shirt was wrinkled, and his unshaven face looked even rougher under the harsh sunlight. He grumbled under his breath, quickly tucking in his shirt and wiping the sweat from his brow. Running a hand through his thinning hair, he tried to make himself look more presentable. It wasn't much of an improvement, but it would have to do.

When Becan's cruiser pulled up to the curb, the crowd surged toward him, their shouts growing louder. People waved their arms, yelling at the sheriff to take action. The atmosphere was tense, bordering on dangerous.

As Becan stepped out of the car, he threw his arms out, trying to project authority. "Alright, alright! Everyone calm down! I hear you."

But the crowd wasn't in a mood to be calmed. They shoved toward him, voices overlapping in a chaotic storm of demands. A man in a dirty baseball cap pushed forward, his face red with anger. "What on earth are you doing, sheriff? People are getting killed, and you're just sitting around!"

Becan narrowed his eyes at the man. "You need to calm down, or I'm going to have to arrest you for disorderly conduct."

The man took another step forward, his fists clenched. "That was my niece who got killed last night! You're not doing enough, Sheriff! You—"

Before he could finish, Becan reached for the man's arm. "That's enough. You're under arrest."

The man swung his arm, trying to shrug off Becan's grip, and in an instant, the situation escalated. The crowd gasped as Becan and the man began to scuffle, pushing and shoving. The deputy rushed over, grabbing the man from behind, and together, they wrestled him to the ground.

"Get off me!" the man shouted, his voice thick with rage and grief. "She's dead because of you!"

The deputy managed to get one cuff on the man's wrist, struggling as he thrashed against them. Becan, panting and red-faced, helped pin the man down as they finally got the second cuff on him.

The crowd watched in stunned silence as the sheriff and deputy hauled the man to his feet and dragged him toward the cruiser. Becan was visibly shaken, but he wasn't about to let the crowd see that. "Anyone else wanna act up?" he called, his voice rough, as he shoved the man into the back of the car.

The crowd murmured in shock, but the arrest had done its job—it quieted them down, if only slightly. Still, there was an undercurrent of anger and fear in the air. They weren't pacified, just waiting.

From the back of the crowd, someone called out, "How about instead of arresting grieving people you get off your ass and go find this creature!"

Becan took a breath, straightened his shirt, and forced a smile. "Look, I've already taken action. The FBI is here."

The murmurs of confusion rippled through the crowd as they listened.

"That's right," Becan continued, seizing the moment. "The FBI is working with my team. We're going to track this thing down and take care of it."

A man near the front raised his voice, still trembling with fear. "What is it, sheriff? What's out there killing people?"

Becan didn't hesitate. "It's an abnormally large wolf," he declared. "Bigger than anything we've seen around here. But don't worry, we've got it under control."

The crowd shifted uneasily, but the mention of the FBI and the sheriff's assurances seemed to calm them, even if only slightly.

"Under control? A young woman got killed last night!," a woman near the back called out.

Becan flashed his well-rehearsed smile. "We had to be sure of what we were dealing with. Now that we know, the FBI is helping us track it down. You're safe now, I promise."

The crowd, though still uneasy, began to disperse. Some people muttered under their breath, but the anger was beginning to ease. For now, it seemed Becan's strategy of arrests and promises had bought him some time.

As the last of the townsfolk drifted away, Becan wiped the

sweat from his brow and turned to his deputy. "Not too bad, huh?"

The deputy glanced nervously at the retreating crowd, then at the man they'd just arrested—the uncle of the girl who had been attacked last night. "Seemed like they were about to tear the place apart."

Becan shrugged. "People just need to feel like someone's in control. We gave 'em that."

Inside the Mayor's office, the receptionist watched through the blinds, her hands still shaking. The sheriff had managed to calm the crowd, but not before arresting the grieving uncle. And while Becan was busy outside, the Mayor had taken the opportunity to slip out the back door, avoiding the angry mob altogether.

By the time Becan made his way into the office, the Mayor was long gone. The receptionist looked up nervously as Becan entered. "The Mayor... he left through the back," she said in a small voice.

Becan wasn't surprised. "Of course, he did," he muttered. "Doesn't want to face the music when things get tough."

The deputy stood by awkwardly. "So... what now?"

Becan smirked, his confidence returning. "Now? Now we sit back and let the FBI do their thing."

He clapped the deputy on the shoulder and headed for the door. "Come on. Let's get an early lunch."

As they left the office, the streets were quiet again, but Becan knew the calm wouldn't last. The fear and anger in the town were like a ticking bomb, and one more attack could send everything spiraling out of control.

But for now, he had managed to keep the townsfolk at bay, and that was enough for him.

THIRTY-FIVE

Jacobi hadn't slept. After they returned to the hotel, he'd closed the blinds and darkened the room, but it hadn't settled him. His mind was too restless to even consider rest.

Jacobi exhaled deeply, running a hand over his face, then picked up his phone from the bedside table. The screen illuminated, casting a faint glow as he scrolled to the latest post. His eyes narrowed as he read the "anonymous" message, each line feeding into the mounting tension he felt.

"Sheriff BACON just ARRESTED Peter Murray, who lost his niece last night!!" one post raged. "How is this even happening?? We're the ones who need protection, and he's arresting a grieving uncle?? Unbelievable!"

The comments were furious, each one angrier than the last. The town was in an uproar. Jacobi scrolled through the replies, seeing that Peter's arrest had sparked a wave of outrage. People were furious that Peter, still grieving the brutal attack on his niece, had been hauled off to jail for confronting the sheriff.

But it wasn't just that.

Eunice Rogers had jumped back into the conversation.

"I'm calling on all who care about this town to arm up and join our nightly watch. The sheriff won't do a damn thing, but we will."

The comments underneath that post were worse. Eunice had stirred up more trouble, recruiting more people into his vigilante group. Jacobi's stomach churned as he read the replies—photos of men and women, armed and ready, eager to hunt down the "killer wolf" that had been terrorizing the town.

Jacobi clenched his fist. This wasn't just a group of scared people anymore. This was a full-blown mob, led by a reckless man who didn't know what he was getting into. These people were going to get themselves killed.

The clock on his phone read 11 a.m. He tossed the phone

onto the bed and paced the room, rubbing his face with his hand. He thought about Eunice's call to arms—the armed men and women patrolling the streets, thinking they could handle a creature that had already claimed lives. They had no idea what they were walking into.

Jacobi glanced into the other room, where Beretti was still sleeping, her breathing steady and deep. He wouldn't wake her. Not yet. She needed rest.

But Jacobi couldn't just sit there anymore. He had to do something. He couldn't let Eunice lead these people straight into danger. The image of armed citizens marching around town, thinking they could take down a creature they didn't understand, flashed through his mind again. It made him sick.

He pulled up the FBI database on his phone, quickly searching for Eunice's address. Once it loaded, he holstered his gun, snatched his jacket and keys, and headed for the door. He wasn't about to sit back and let Eunice stir up more trouble. This had to end—now.

- - - - - - - - - - -

The sun was already high in the sky when Jacobi's SUV rumbled to life. He eased out of the lot and set his course for

Eunice's place on the outskirts of town.

The drive gave him time to think, to prepare himself. He knew Eunice wouldn't be easy to deal with. The man lived for this kind of drama, always eager to assert his authority and rile people up. Jacobi had seen Eunice's type before—paranoid, reckless, and dangerous in the worst way.

As Jacobi turned down the dirt road leading to Eunice's property, he could see the house ahead, worn down from years of neglect. The roof sagged slightly, and the paint had peeled away in places, revealing the bare wood beneath. The lawn was overgrown, and old tools were strewn across the front yard, rusted and forgotten.

Jacobi parked out front and turned off the engine. He could see an old Ford pickup parked beside the house. Eunice was home.

He got out of the car and walked to the front door with determination. This wasn't going to be a polite conversation. Eunice needed to be shut down before things got worse.

Jacobi knocked on the door, the sound echoing through the otherwise silent yard. As he waited, he glanced around, taking in the scattered beer bottles and crushed cans littering the porch and yard—signs of long nights and rowdy gatherings.

Footsteps approached from inside, and after a few moments, the door creaked open to reveal Eunice: a short white man around forty, his unkempt hair and faded, grease-stained T-shirt underscoring a rough, almost defiant look.

"What do you want?" Eunice growled, his voice edged with distrust.

Jacobi took a step forward, his tone firm. "We need to talk about your little rally and the vigilante group you've been stirring up."

Eunice leaned against the doorframe, arms crossed, his brow furrowing. "Who the hell are you?"

Jacobi pulled out his badge. "Special Agent Noah Jacobi. FBI."

The moment the words left Jacobi's mouth, Eunice's expression changed. His eyes darkened, and a scowl twisted his face. "FBI, huh?" His voice dripped with disdain. "Figures they'd send in some pretty boy Fed to try and shut us down."

Jacobi didn't flinch. "I'm here to stop you from getting people killed, Eunice. You don't understand what you're dealing with."

Eunice's anger flared. He straightened up, his fists clenched at his sides. "I know exactly what I'm dealing with—a damn wolf that's tearing apart this town. And if the useless sheriff won't stop it, we will."

Jacobi stood his ground, keeping his voice steady. "It's not just a wolf. And going out there with guns, with no plan, is going to make this worse. People are going to die."

Eunice stepped forward, his face red with fury. "You think you can come here and tell me how to protect my town? I don't need some Fed telling me what to do. You FBI types never do anything but sit in your offices while we're out here fighting for our lives."

Jacobi held up a hand, trying to calm the situation before it escalated. "I'm not your enemy, Eunice. But if you keep pushing this, you're going to lead those people right into danger. This thing isn't what you think it is."

But Eunice wasn't listening anymore. His face twisted into a sneer as he stepped back, yelling, "Get the fuck off my porch!" Then he slammed the door in Jacobi's face, the sound echoing through the yard.

THIRTY-SIX

The motel room door creaked open, and Jacobi stepped inside, the unease from his visit with Eunice still clinging to him. He hadn't even had time to take off his jacket when Beretti's voice cut through the silence, sharp and unmistakably angry.

"Jacobi."

He turned to see her standing in the doorway between their rooms, arms crossed, eyes narrowed. She didn't need to ask where he'd been—Eunice had made sure of that. The man had already posted on social media, bragging about the FBI showing up at his door and how neither the sheriff nor the Feds could shut him up.

Jacobi braced himself. He could feel the frustration radiating off Beretti, and he knew he'd messed up.

"What were you thinking?" Beretti demanded, her voice low but filled with irritation. "You went to see Eunice without even consulting me. Let alone taking me with you."

Jacobi sighed, running a hand over his face. He should've known this would blow back on him. "I was trying to stop him before things got worse," he said, his tone defensive. "You were asleep. I didn't want to wake you."

"That's not the point," Beretti shot back. "We're supposed to be a team, Jacobi. You don't just run off and handle things on your own without backup. Especially with someone like Eunice. You looked up his address so you would have seen his criminal history. He is not someone you mess with by yourself, particularly as you are FBI and he has a hard on for Feds."

He shook his head, already regretting how he'd handled things. "Look, I thought I could de-escalate the situation before it spiraled out of control."

Beretti stepped closer, her eyes locking onto his. "And how did that work out for you? Did you stop him? Or did you just make things worse?"

Jacobi's head dropped slightly. He knew the answer, and he hated it. "Eunice is stubborn," he muttered. "But I didn't want to wait and let him stir up more trouble."

Beretti took a deep breath, softening her tone but not her frustration. "Noah, you've got to stop doing this. I get that you want to fix things, that you think acting quickly is the answer, but you're not in this alone. We're a team. You can't just keep running off and handling things by yourself."

He dropped onto the side of the bed, his hands gripping the edge as he looked down. "I know. It's just... I see things going sideways, and I can't just sit around waiting. I want to do something."

"Yeah, and that's the problem," Beretti said, sitting down across from him. "You've got this instinct to rush in and fix everything yourself. You're not a lone soldier. You've got a partner, and you need to trust that I've got your back."

Her words hit him harder than he expected. She wasn't wrong, and deep down, he knew it. Jacobi had always been the type to act first, think later—something that worked in the military, where split-second decisions could mean the difference between life and death. But in their line of work now, it didn't always help.

"You're right," he admitted, his voice quieter now. "I should've consulted you."

Beretti nodded, a small smile tugging at the corner of her lips. "You damn well should've. But you're here now. We've got a job to do, and we need to be on the same page. Next time, you bring me in before you charge off, okay?"

Jacobi chuckled lightly. "Okay. Deal."

Their conversation hung in the air, and they both sat silently for a moment. It was a reminder for both of them—this wasn't just about stopping cryptids or tracking down monsters. It was about trust, about working together as a team. And for Jacobi, it was about learning to share the burden, even when his instincts told him otherwise.

Perry's truck pulled up just as Beretti glanced at her phone.

"Oh, perfect timing," Jacobi said, grabbing his gear.

Beretti smirked. "Yeah, we were just going to go without you if you didn't show."

Jacobi stopped, raising an eyebrow. "Really?"

Beretti laughed, giving his shoulder a pat. "No, not really."

They all piled into the truck, settling in as Perry shifted into gear. As they headed out, Jacobi quickly filled him in on his tense encounter with Eunice, who'd been about as receptive as anticipated. Perry listened with a tired but focused expression, nodding as he navigated out of town.

"That figures. I wouldn't expect the likes of Eunice to make things easy," Perry stated.

"Oh, before I forget," Perry began, looking over at Beretti and Jacobi, "we had a bit of a scene outside the Mayor's office this morning. A crowd gathered, demanding answers about the attacks, and the sheriff stepped out to try and calm them down."

Jacobi leaned forward. "The Mayor actually addressed it?"

Perry shook his head. "Nope. Mayor claimed he had 'urgent business' and stayed out of sight, leaving the sheriff to handle things alone."

With a skeptical look, Beretti tilted her head. "And the crowd just accepted that?"

"Not exactly," Perry continued. "Peter Ramsey—the uncle of the young woman attacked last night—was there, and he got fired up. Started shouting that people had a right to know what was going on." He paused, a faint look of frustration on his face. "The sheriff tried to defuse it but lost patience. Things got heated, and he ended up arresting Peter for 'disorderly conduct,' though it seemed more like a move to save face."

Beretti looked incredulous. "He arrested the guy for demanding answers about his own niece?"

"Yeah, pretty much," Perry said, his voice edged with irritation. "He only let him go after the Mayor leaned on him hard enough. Seems like keeping up appearances means more to them than helping people."

Jacobi shook his head, looking out the window. "So, the sheriff's more focused on control than actually doing his job. What a stand-up guy."

Perry nodded. "That's exactly it. But if they keep this up, it'll blow up in their faces soon enough. The crowd's only getting louder, and before long, we'll have more than just angry townsfolk banging on the Mayor's door if we don't find this thing fast."

Jacobi gave Perry a questioning look. "How the hell is the sheriff still in office?"

Perry glanced back at him. "Friends in high places, my friend."

THIRTY-SEVEN

Perry drove them toward the trailhead, each of them lost in their own thoughts. Under different circumstances, the forest's beauty might have been calming—the way sunlight filtered through the canopy. But today, every darkened hollow and thicket seemed watchful, hiding secrets they were unwilling to give up. Beretti kept her eyes on the trees, noting every break in the foliage from the passenger seat, while Jacobi sat in the back, leaning forward tensely, his gaze fixed on the passing woods.

They were about a mile out when Perry suddenly hit the brakes, the truck jerking to a halt. "Sorry, guys," he muttered as he threw it into reverse. Perry backed up along the road, stopping when a half-hidden blue pickup truck came into view, nestled in the brush.

"Well, I'll be damned. That's Tucker Leney's truck," Perry said, nodding toward it as he parked. "Looks like he tried to tuck it away in the trees."

They climbed out and approached the pickup, moving cautiously not knowing what or who they would find. Jacobi peeked in the driver's window, finding the interior well-kept and empty, save for a few empty candy wrappers and an old coffee cup in the holder. Circling the truck, Beretti scanned the ground around it, searching for any signs of a struggle, any clue as to why Tucker and Bo had left it here. It was just a truck, hidden away, with little else to go on.

"Well," Perry muttered, squinting through the dense forest ahead, trying to catch sight of any path. "At least we have a starting point now."

Jacobi nodded, glancing back at the deserted road. "Looks like they were trying to stay off anyone's radar."

Perry pulled out his phone, checking the map. "The creek's only about a mile in from here."

While Perry studied the map, Beretti's gaze fell on a faint line of flattened grass and disturbed dirt leading into the forest. She crouched down, tracing the faint track with her hand. "Looks like a worn trail heading out from here," she said, glancing up. "Might be recent."

They exchanged a look, a silent agreement passing between them. Jacobi went back to the cruiser, opening the case holding their high-powered rifles. They each took one, loading the magazines and securing their packs, feeling the rifles' solid and reassuring heft in their hands. Perry adjusted his grip, casting a look of steely resolve at his partners.

"You know the drill. Stay close, and keep quiet," he murmured.

Without another word, they moved onto the narrow trail, weaving cautiously past the tall Douglas firs. The forest thickened around them, growing darker with each step as they followed the faint path winding toward Norris Creek. Rifles at the ready, every sense was sharpened, attuned to the forest's every sound.

THIRTY-EIGHT

As they ventured deeper into the forest, Beretti paused every so often, scanning for signs they were still on the right track—an overturned stone, a broken branch, disturbed foliage. The shadows around them grew thicker, and an eerie silence hung in the air; even the usual sounds of birds had vanished.

After a while, Jacobi lifted his head, sniffing the air. A look of disgust crossed his face as he glanced at the others. "Damn! Do you guys smell that?"

Beretti brought a hand to her nose, her expression twisting as the foul stench hit her. "Yeah... that's strong."

"That's decomposition," Perry confirmed, in a hushed

tone. He scanned the area ahead, his eyes narrowed. "Not too far off."

They followed the sickening scent, moving slowly. Each of them was bracing for what lay ahead, though none of them expected the scene they found in a small clearing a few yards away.

Two bodies lay strewn across the ground, or what was left of them. Torn flesh and shredded clothing covered the earth, and limbs lay twisted and broken around the clearing. Blood stained the grass and trees, dried dark on the ground, with pieces of flesh scattered amidst the underbrush. Perry knelt down, taking in the grisly scene with a look of grim recognition.

"That looks like two bodies," Perry muttered, glancing around the grisly scene, his eyes narrowing as he took in the scattered remains.

Beretti observed the insects for a moment before standing up. "The presence of both flies and these beetles suggests the bodies have been here about a week. That lines up with when Tucker and Bo went missing right?"

Jacobi frowned glancing at the beetles. "How do you know that?"

Beretti smirked slightly. "I took a forensic entomology course back in training. Thought it might come in handy."

Jacobi nodded, visibly impressed, as Perry looked back at the bodies.

Perry sighed, the grim reality sinking in. He straightened, scanning the forest around them as if bracing for something to emerge from the thickening darkness beyond.

"These men were obliterated," Jacobi murmured, his voice tight.

Beretti swept her eyes over the area trying to take in every detail. She moved about thirty yards from the bodies, where something unusual caught her eye. "Hey, over here!" she called, motioning for the others.

Perry and Jacobi joined her, and immediately saw what she'd found: another body, but this one wasn't human. It lay crumpled in a pile, fur matted with blood and limbs twisted in unnatural angles. Even in death, the creature was monstrous—a juvenile Dogman, its leg caught in a large bear trap. Its eyes were dull and empty, its face locked in a feral snarl. The stench of decomposition hung thick around it, adding to the somber scene.

Beretti crouched down beside the creature, examining the

trap. "This poor thing did everything it could to get out of the trap," she said softly, her fingers tracing the iron teeth biting into its leg. "Probably died of exhaustion or blood loss."

Jacobi tilted his head, studying the lifeless creature. "So… wait. This Dogman couldn't have killed the men."

Beretti shook her head, a pensive look crossing her face as she studied the scene. "No, this one's been dead about as long as Tucker and Bo. Something else killed them. Maybe the Dogman we're after. It might have found this young one trapped and…" She hesitated, glancing over the brutal remains. "Maybe it killed them out of rage."

Perry's eyes shifted to the trees, his hand tightening around his rifle. "You think it was a pack mate? Something that saw the young one trapped and went after the men for revenge?"

Beretti nodded slowly, lost in thought. "It's possible. I wonder if Tucker and Bo were trying to trap a grizzly—or if they were just stupid enough to try trapping one of these things."

Jacobi adjusted his grip on his rifle, scanning the tree line. "Did you know Tucker and Bo were into illegal trapping, Chief?"

Perry shook his head. "No, I didn't. Could have been the big payday they were telling their friends about. Apparently, they'd been raking in cash the last few months, but Tucker told a buddy he thought he was in too deep."

Beretti glanced at Perry, her eyes narrowing. "That sounds like they were involved with someone else."

"Yeah, it does," Perry replied, swatting a fly away from his face. "I'll call in the coroner, Fish and Game and get a few deputies out here to help transport the Dogman carcass. I'm guessing your bosses will want to take it in?"

"They will," Beretti said, nodding.

THIRTY-NINE

The clearing was quiet as Doc Whitmore arrived with his crime scene technicians and a few deputies. They moved with grim purpose, setting up equipment and photographing the grisly scene. Doc Whitmore, a tall, wiry man with a perpetual frown, crouched beside the remains of one man, his eyes sharp as he examined the shredded flesh and torn limbs.

A gust of wind picked up, carrying the stench of decomposition straight at the technicians. No matter how many times they'd worked around dead bodies, it was a smell they never got used to. One by one, they pulled masks from their kits, covering their noses and mouths, but even the fabric did little to dull the putrid odor that hung thick in the air.

Whitmore continued his inspection, noting the familiar pattern of claw marks and bite wounds on the remains. After a moment, he straightened, pulled off his gloves, and walked over to the juvenile Dogman's body tangled in the trap. With a dry tone, he muttered, "Well, that makes sense. It wasn't any ordinary wolf responsible for all of this."

Just then, Warden Harvey Acosta arrived followed by two deputies, their presence announced by the crackle of branches as the Warden pulled a hunter's game sled through the underbrush. A seasoned wildlife officer with a rugged, weathered face, Acosta came to a halt, his eyes locking onto the Dogman's body. He blinked in disbelief, then looked at Perry, then back to the creature, his mouth half-open as he took in the massive claws, the muscular frame, and the face twisted in a final, feral snarl.

"What... what is this?" he murmured, almost to himself, as he took a cautious step closer. Acosta had encountered his share of predators in these woods, but nothing could have prepared him for the nightmare sprawled before him.

Perry joined him, his tone calm but serious. "It's exactly what it looks like, Harvey. They call it a 'Dogman.'"

Acosta's eyes widened in disbelief. "What the fuck is a Dogman?" he asked, glancing back and forth between Perry and the creature's hulking, lifeless body.

"It's a cryptid," Perry answered flatly.

Acosta shook his head, looking from the creature's massive body to Perry, his voice rising with disbelief. "This... this thing doesn't look like any dog. It looks like a freakin' deformed werewolf, Perry!"

"As hard as it is to believe, it's probably best if you don't call this one in Harvey," Perry advised. No official reports, no documentation."

Acosta looked up sharply, still struggling to comprehend what he was seeing. "Are you serious? I'm just supposed to pretend this... this thing doesn't exist?" He looked back down at the Dogman, his mouth set in a tight grimace. The creature's lifeless eyes stared up, its body twisted in the trap, with massive claws and muscular limbs that defied any rational explanation.

Perry nodded, his tone firm but understanding. "Believe me, I'd like people to know what's really out here, Harvey so they can protect themselves and know what they're dealing with. But on the other hand..." He looked around at the others, choosing his words carefully. "If word got out about this... you'd have people pouring into these woods trying to hunt it down. And too many of them would end up like Tucker and Bo."

Acosta considered this, the disbelief still clear in his eyes but tempered with understanding. "Fine. No report. But, damn, Perry… I don't know what to make of this."

Perry placed a reassuring hand on Acosta's shoulder. "None of us do. Just do what you can. Help us get this thing out of here."

Acosta took a deep breath, then pulled out a heavy-duty tarp he'd brought for the job. Perry, Jacobi, and Beretti slipped on gloves, joining him to carefully lift the Dogman's body onto the tarp. Working together, they wrapped the creature tightly, ensuring it was fully covered and secured. Acosta tied the tarp with thick ropes, knotting them firmly to prevent any movement.

With the creature's body finally secured on the sled, Perry, Acosta, and Jacobi took their positions along the edges, bracing for the exhausting task ahead. Together, they began the slow, laborious trek back through the dense forest, the sled's heavy weight snagging on roots and rough patches of ground. Beretti stayed close, stepping in to free the sled each time it got caught.

Nearby, deputies worked to help the crime scene techs carry Tucker and Bo's remains to the coroner's van.

The once-peaceful clearing was now a place forever marred by violence, and with each yard they moved, it was as though the forest grew darker, the silence around them deeper and more unnerving.

After what felt like an eternity, they reached the edge of the forest. Perry paused to take a deep breath, then looked back at the others. "We'll debrief later. For now, let's just get this done. And remember… no one needs to know more than they have to."

Doc Whitmore, his technicians, Acosta, and the deputies all nodded, Perry's words hanging heavily in the air. They knew, as they walked back to the vehicles, that they were leaving with more than just evidence—they were leaving with a secret none of them fully understood, but each was bound to keep.

The juvenile Dogman was carefully loaded into Perry's truck, its bulk barely contained within the bed, covered tightly with tarps. The stench of decay lingered, an unsettling reminder of everything they'd uncovered. As Perry secured the tailgate, Beretti stepped up beside him.

"Agents will meet us at the sheriff's office to retrieve the Dogman," she said, her voice steady despite the unease in her eyes.

Perry nodded, glancing back at the others. He had found the missing men, but now even more questions demanded answers.

They climbed into the vehicle, each feeling the gravity of what they'd just witnessed as they drove back to town, the darkened woods fading in the rearview mirrors behind them.

FORTY

By 8 p.m., Jacobi and Beretti had grabbed a quick meal and were back on the road, patrolling the quiet streets. They knew they were dealing with a creature likely bent on revenge, making it even more unpredictable and dangerous.

As they cruised through the dimly lit town, the streets lay empty, almost unnervingly quiet. At a stop sign, Jacobi checked in with Perry, who was patrolling the opposite side of town with another deputy. Just as he lowered the radio, Jacobi cocked his head, frowning as he listened. "You hear that?"

Beretti paused, focusing. A faint, irregular popping sound echoed from a distance. Her eyes sharpened. "Yeah.

Gunshots."

Jacobi pressed down on the accelerator, preparing to turn toward the direction of the shots when a flash of movement cut across their headlights—a dark, hulking figure sprinting at an impossible speed, crossing the street and vanishing into the darkness ahead.

"What the..." Jacobi muttered, reaching for his door handle, about to jump out and give chase.

"Wait!" Beretti grabbed his arm, stopping him. "You won't catch it on foot. Not at that speed."

Seconds later, the crack of more gunshots echoed down the street. They spotted a group of figures running toward them, their rifles raised as they fired wildly at the fleeing creature. It was Eunice and his posse, hell-bent on hunting the Dogman. The creature was already far ahead, well out of their reach, but the men kept firing, bullets ricocheting off street signs and walls.

The Dogman vanished behind a house, too fast for them. The group stopped at the end of the street, and Jacobi drove toward them, pulling up beside the mob. He and Beretti stepped out of the SUV to confront Eunice and his men.

Jacobi stormed up to Eunice, his voice laced with

irritation. "What the hell are you doing, Eunice? Shooting off rounds in the dark like that—you're going to get someone killed."

Eunice smirked, not bothering to lower his gun. "Aw, I didn't know I'd have to answer to *you*, Agent. Ain't like you Feds have done jack squat since you got here. Hell, we're just speeding things along."

"By firing wildly? You're putting the whole town at risk," Jacobi shot back, his frustration boiling over. "Stop acting like this is your personal war zone."

Eunice snorted, eyes glinting. "Oh, and you're the expert, huh? 'Mr. Big-Shot Agent' here to save us all? You wouldn't know what to do with this thing if it was spoon-fed to you. We'll handle it *our way,* and you can keep your nose out of it."

"Your way is reckless," Jacobi spat. "You've got people out here scared and waving guns around without a damn clue. You're not handling it—you're making it worse."

"Better than waitin' around for some fancy Fed to do *nothin',*" Eunice shot back, voice dripping with sarcasm. "You want to lecture me? Go on back to your cushy SUV and let us handle this."

Before Jacobi could respond, a scream tore through the

night, silencing everyone. The smirk fell from Eunice's face as the reality set in.

"Over there!" a woman cried, pointing with a trembling hand down the block.

Everyone turned in unison, and at the end of the street, partially hidden behind a parked car, stood the creature. Its hulking frame was barely visible in the dim light, but the amber glow of its eyes betrayed its presence.

Then, a deep, guttural growl rumbled from down the street, so powerful and resonant that everyone felt it vibrate in their chests. The sound seemed to sink into their bones, freezing them where they stood.

The crowd gasped, a wave of fear rippling through them as the growl echoed down the empty street. For a moment, everything was still.

Then chaos erupted.

Eunice, driven by a mix of adrenaline, stupidity and bravado, broke from the group and charged toward the creature, leading half the posse in a reckless dash. Gunshots rang out, bullets flying wildly as they fired into the night.

Some of the men in the group stood frozen, their feet

rooted to the pavement as they watched in disbelief.

"Stop! Stop shooting!" Beretti yelled, her voice lost in the chaotic burst of gunfire.

"Everyone, back off!" Jacobi shouted, but his warning fell on deaf ears as Eunice and his group surged forward, still firing.

The creature snarled, ducking behind the parked car with lightning speed, evading the bullets. Moving in a blur, it disappeared into the darkness just as Eunice's group reached the car, their weapons still raised, breaths ragged with the rush of adrenaline.

"Imbeciles," Jacobi muttered, sprinting toward them, Beretti close behind. "You're going to get someone killed!"

As they reached the mob, Jacobi grabbed the nearest man by the arm and yanked him back. "Put the guns down! Now!" he barked, his voice cutting through the chaos.

The men gradually slowed, lowering their guns, their breathing jagged. Eunice, standing at the front of the group, glared defiantly, still clutching his rifle. His eyes were wide, a mix of fear and stubbornness flashing across his face.

Beretti stepped in front of the group, raising her hands in

a calming gesture. "Let's all take a deep breath and calm down."

The chaos began to settle, though the men's and women's faces remained pale, their hands shaking. Jacobi scanned the area, searching the front yards for any sign of movement, but the creature had slipped away, leaving behind only fear and confusion.

Eunice, catching his breath, suddenly puffed up his chest, trying to regain his composure. "I shot it," he declared, glancing around at the crowd for validation. "I swear I hit it in the leg. Did anyone see it limping?"

A few of the men nodded uncertainly, while others stayed silent, too shaken to speak.

Beretti stepped forward, her tone direct. "Eunice, there's no proof you hit it. All you did was create chaos and put everyone in danger."

Eunice scoffed, trying to save face. "I know I hit it—I saw it flinch."

She locked eyes with him. "If you did hit it, then it's wounded, and that means it's even more dangerous now. Injured predators don't run; they fight. So next time, think before firing off like that."

Her words hung in the air, the reality sinking in as the group fell silent.

Eunice shifted, his bluster fading as Beretti's words settled. He turned to Jacobi, voice low but sharp with anxiety. "So what the heck is this thing, Agent? 'Cause that ain't no damn wolf."

Jacobi met his stare, dead serious. "We told you already— it's something different, something none of you are prepared to face. You keep going off half-cocked like this, and it'll pick you all off, one by one."

Eunice scoffed, trying to save face, though his voice shook slightly. "Big talk for a Fed. Maybe you think you know what's best, but it's our town, and if it's out there, we'll be the ones to end it."

As the scene heated, an older woman suddenly emerged from one of the houses. With ratty hair and wearing only a nightgown, she clutched a large cross to her chest and stood on her porch, looking out over the crowd.

"I saw it! It was the devil! You're all in danger!" she yelled, her voice breaking through the night air.

One of the townsfolk rolled his eyes and shouted back, "Shut the fuck up, Bernice!"

Beretti turned to her, raising a hand with an air of calm authority. "Ma'am, please, head back inside and lock your door. We're going to take care of it."

She huffed but, muttering under her breath, shuffled back inside and closed the door, casting one last wary glance at the crowd.

Before anyone else could speak, the sudden roar of an engine echoed down the street. A cruiser pulled up, screeching its tires as it pulled to a hard stop. Perry stepped out, another deputy at his side. His face was tense as he took in the scene, his eyes moving from the armed crowd to Jacobi and Beretti.

"What the hell happened here?" Perry asked, his voice sharp.

Jacobi gestured toward the group. "They saw the creature and decided to chase it down. Fired a bunch of wild rounds, but it got away."

Perry's expression hardened as he looked out over the group. "We definitely don't need a bunch of trigger-happy vigilantes chasing a dangerous creature through town." His eyes narrowed, taking in their anxious faces and trembling hands, each still gripping a rifle. "Alright," he said sharply.

"Let's get everyone out of here before somebody gets seriously hurt."

He gave the crowd a stern look. "And one more thing," he added, his voice cold. "If I find any property damaged by stray bullets, every one of you will be held accountable. We're here to protect this town, not destroy it."

Jacobi stepped forward, his voice carrying across the tense silence. "You've done enough tonight. Go home, lock your doors, and let us take it from here."

There was some grumbling, but the townsfolk had no argument left. They began to disperse, heads lowered and shoulders slumped, fear and frustration etched on every face.

There was some grumbling, but no one argued. One by one, the townsfolk began to disperse, shoulders slumped, faces etched with lingering fear and frustration.

Eunice lingered at the back, his eyes fixed on Jacobi. "We're not done, you know," he said, in a hushed tone.

Jacobi met his gaze evenly. "You're damn right we're not. But next time, don't make it worse."

Eunice held Jacobi's stare for a moment, then turned and stalked off, rifle slung over his shoulder.

Perry watched him go, then turned back to Jacobi and Beretti. "This is getting out of control. We need to shut this down before it turns into a bloodbath."

Beretti glanced toward the perimeter of the woods, her jaw set. "It's not going to stop until we stop it."

Jacobi nodded grimly, glancing at Perry. "And we better do it fast."

FORTY-ONE

Eunice slammed the door of his beat-up pickup truck, muttering under his breath as he settled into the driver's seat. "FBI bitch doesn't know what she's talking about," he growled, jabbing the key into the ignition. "I hit that thing—I know I did." His hands trembled slightly as he started the engine, and the old truck rumbled to life.

He shot a glare at the rearview mirror, imagining Beretti's smug face staring back at him. "I don't need no Feds to tell me what's out there. I hit it, and it's gonna limp into the forest like a whipped dog," he mumbled, shaking his head. His hatred for law enforcement boiled just beneath the surface, simmering into anger. "Don't need no damn FBI around here. We've been takin' care of ourselves just fine."

Eunice threw the truck into gear and peeled out of the parking lot, the tires screeching. As he sped down the empty road toward home, his mind wasn't on the road—he was still mumbling to himself, gripping the steering wheel tighter with every mile. "Feds don't know squat... damned wolves, we'll shoot every last one of them."

The road twisted and turned as Eunice drove deeper into the rural outskirts, the trees closing in on either side. His headlights cut through the inky blackness, but the deeper he drove, the darker the night seemed to become. His muttering continued, a steady stream of complaints about the FBI, the sheriff, and anyone else who thought they could tell him what to do.

As the truck neared his driveway, something caught his eye. A shape—low to the ground, dark, and still—was sitting in the middle of the road. Eunice instinctively slowed the truck, squinting through the windshield to make out what it was. His heart gave a sudden, uneasy lurch, but he quickly shoved the feeling down.

"Damn deer," he muttered, but his voice wavered slightly.

The figure in the road wasn't a deer.

It was low to the ground, hunched, and its fur gleamed

under the headlights. Eunice's grip on the steering wheel tightened, his bravado faltering for the first time since the encounter with Beretti and Jacobi.

Without thinking, he hit the horn. "Get outta the road!" he shouted, but the words felt hollow in the night air.

The creature moved.

It rose slowly to its full height, unfolding its massive body in a way that made Eunice's skin crawl. Then its head turned, and its glowing amber eyes locked onto him. It wasn't scared. It wasn't running away.

Eunice felt a knot of fear form in his gut as he slammed the truck into reverse, his foot heavy on the gas. The tires squealed as he tried to put distance between himself and the creature, but before he could fully react, it charged. The impact came with terrifying speed—the Dogman slammed into the side of the truck with enough force to send it swerving wildly.

"Jesus Christ!" Eunice shouted, gripping the wheel as he fought to control the truck. The engine roared as he pressed the gas, but the Dogman wasn't finished.

With a heavy thud, the creature leaped into the truck bed, its weight making the entire vehicle lurch. Eunice's heart raced as he glanced into the rearview mirror—those amber eyes stared back at him, closer than ever. The Dogman crouched, claws scraping across the metal, its lips curling back into a snarl.

"It's a fucking werewolf!" Eunice screamed, throwing the truck into drive and flooring the gas.

The Dogman stayed on the truck bed for several terrifying seconds before leaping off and disappearing into the trees. Eunice's hands trembled as he fought to keep the truck on the road, his eyes darting between the rearview mirror and the pitch-black woods around him.

He hadn't noticed the ditch until it was too late, the truck lurching forward as the front tires sank deep into the mud. Eunice cursed under his breath, slamming on the gas, but the wheels only spun uselessly, spraying dirt. Frustrated and panicked, he threw the door open and scrambled out, grabbing his rifle from the passenger seat.

Stumbling onto the road, he spun in a frenzied circle, firing blindly into the darkness. Each shot cracked through the night, his voice echoing after it, hoarse and desperate. "You don't scare me!" he yelled, the words spilling out in a wild attempt to silence the fear clawing at his chest. "Come on, then! Come on!" he shouted, squeezing the trigger again and again, firing until the rifle clicked empty. He stood there, chest heaving, his eyes darting frantically across the tree line. Silence closed in around him, thick and unmoving, and his bravado faltered, leaving him stranded in the quiet that stretched endlessly ahead.

"Stay calm... stay calm..." Eunice muttered, gripping the rifle as he backed away from the wreck. His house was just ahead—if he could make it inside, he'd be safe.

The walk to the house felt like a lifetime, each step heavier than the last. The sound of his boots hitting the dirt echoed as he took shallow gasps of breath. The air felt thick, like he was moving through molasses. The woods, which had once seemed so familiar, now loomed over him like a predator waiting to strike.

Eunice's heart was pounding in his chest by the time he reached his front door. He flung it open and slammed it shut behind him, locking it with trembling hands. For a few moments, he stood there in the darkness of his home, trying to catch his breath.

But something felt off.

He glanced at the windows, at the darkness beyond the glass. It was too quiet. The woods had gone silent—no wind, no rustling leaves, no sounds of wildlife. Just... nothing.

"Looks like I scared it off," he muttered to himself.

Despite his false bravado, a cold chill ran down his spine as he looked around his house. It was in a state of disrepair, something he'd never cared much about. The front door barely stayed on its hinges, and the windows rattled with the slightest breeze. He knew, deep down, that if the creature wanted in, there was nothing stopping it. His house wouldn't hold up. Hell, if someone blew on the front door hard enough, it might fall over.

"It's all good," he whispered, striving to hide his rising panic. "It'll hold." But the words felt hollow in the silence.

He forced himself toward the kitchen, grabbing a cold beer from the fridge and cracking it open with a shaky hand. After a swig, he reached for a box of ammo from the cabinet, loading each round with a sense of grim determination. Finally, he took a heavy seat in his recliner, placing the rifle within arm's reach.

Taking another long gulp of beer, he settled into the darkened room, eyes fixed on the front door. If that thing came back, he'd be ready. Just as his heart rate began to slow, a faint scraping noise broke through the silence.

Eunice froze, his eyes darting toward the front window. At the edge of the driveway stood the creature, its massive form barely illuminated by the dim porch light. It reached out a clawed hand and slowly scraped its nails down the length of his letterbox, the metallic screech sending a shiver through him. The deliberate, taunting gesture left deep gouges in the metal, and Eunice's breath caught in his throat as he watched, unable to tear his gaze away.

His mind was going a million miles an hour. He slowly reached for his rifle, every inch of him screaming to run, but there was nowhere to go. He was trapped. His fingers trembled around the rifle, but it felt useless in his hands now.

Then he heard heavy footsteps. On his porch. Slow, deliberate.

Eunice got up and braced himself near the door, his heart hammering in his chest. "Come on, you bastard," he muttered, though his voice wavered.

Then, without warning, the door burst inward.

The impact knocked Eunice off his feet, sending him crashing to the ground. His rifle clattered across the floor, just out of reach. As he scrambled to get up, the hulking figure of the beast filled the doorway, its claws scraping against the wood, its breath coming out in slow, deliberate growls.

Eunice tried to crawl backward, but the Dogman was faster. It lunged, pinning him to the floor with a heavy paw, its claws digging into his chest. Pain shot through him, but it was the fear—the absolute, paralyzing fear—that left him breathless.

The creature leaned in, its snout inches from his face. He could feel its hot breath, smell the rancid stench of death on it. The creature's lips curled back into something that almost resembled a smile, as if it knew exactly how terrified Eunice was.

And then, in one swift motion, the beast struck.

Its jaws closed around Eunice's face, ripping into his lips and nose with brutal force. Blood poured from the gaping wound, soaking his shirt and pooling beneath him. The creature snarled, claws tearing into his chest and abdomen, leaving nothing but devastation in its wake.

Eunice's body jerked violently as the life drained out of him. His mind, fogged with pain and terror, grasped at the last flicker of consciousness, but it was no use.

The creature tore at him with primal ferocity, its hunger unrelenting. It wasn't just killing him—it was eating him, ripping flesh from bone in brutal, savage bites. The creature's jaws snapped and tore, blood splattering the walls and floor as it devoured Eunice, the sound of tearing flesh filling the small room.

In the end, Eunice lay in a broken, ravaged heap. His flesh and organs were scattered, bones cracked and chewed on. The creature, its amber eyes still gleaming, stood over its meal, its breath heavy, its hunger temporarily sated.

Leaving only devastation and the remnants of Eunice Rogers, the creature disappeared into the night after taking one last look at the chaos it had created.

FORTY-TWO

Beretti, Jacobi, and Perry lingered by their vehicles, watching the last vigilante stragglers disappear into the darkened streets.

"I doubt we'll see the Dogman in town again tonight," Jacobi said, leaning against the hood of the SUV. His face was still tense from the chaos earlier, but his voice had an edge of confidence to it.

"Yeah, it caused enough trouble for one night," Perry agreed, rubbing the back of his neck. "I just hope it stays out in the woods.

Beretti scanned the horizon, her sharp gaze cutting through the night. "We need to be careful, though. This thing... it's smarter than your average predator. It won't just attack when we expect it."

Just as they were starting to relax, the unmistakable sound of an engine approached. A cruiser rolled up, its lights cutting through the dark. Perry raised his brow as the car parked nearby. The door opened, and out stepped Sheriff Becan, looking as disheveled as ever, but trying to project an air of authority.

Everyone exchanged glances, surprised that Becan had bothered to show up. It was unlike him to appear during an actual crisis, especially this late.

"Sheriff," Perry greeted, trying to mask his confusion.

Becan strolled over, his belly protruding slightly as he walked, his shirt as wrinkled as ever. He had a cigarette dangling from his mouth, the ash desperately holding on. With a casual air, he took a long drag, exhaling slowly as he approached.

"What brings you out here?" Beretti asked, her tone laced with curiosity.

The sheriff puffed out his chest, looking like he was trying to assume command. "I'm doing my job little lady," he said, with a tone of self-importance that was so out of place it made everyone pause.

There was a beat of silence before Jacobi coughed, trying to cover a laugh. Perry's face darkened, clearly annoyed at the sheriff's patronizing tone.

"Her name is Special Agent Beretti," Perry muttered, exchanging a look with Beretti.

But Sheriff Becan didn't seem to notice or care. He squared his shoulders, clearly expecting everyone to fall in line. "I've been handling things just fine, thank you very much," he added, as if reminding them that he was still the sheriff. "Just wanted to make sure you all had things under control."

Beretti had to bite her lip to stop from laughing. The absurdity of Becan acting like he'd been in control this whole time was almost too much. But she played along, nodding slowly. "Well, we appreciate the... support."

Oblivious to their amusement, Becan took another drag from his cigarette and nodded. "Good. You agents just let me know if you need anything," he said, as if he hadn't been avoiding them since they arrived.

Jacobi, still suppressing a grin, nodded. "Will do, sheriff."

Perry, unable to resist, added, "You've really been on top of things tonight, huh?"

Becan puffed his chest out a bit more. "Of course. Always am."

As the sheriff sauntered off, Beretti, Jacobi, and Perry exchanged glances, barely able to contain their laughter.

"Well," Jacobi said with a grin, "that was... something."

Perry chuckled, though his annoyance lingered. "Yeah, if by 'doing his job,' he means showing up late and pretending he's been in charge the whole time."

Beretti shook her head. "He's a real piece of work, isn't he?"

Perry sighed, the moment of levity fading. "Let's just hope we don't need him to do more than puff his chest out. We've got enough on our plates without him getting in the way."

Jacobi nodded. "More of a hindrance than help."

As the night deepened, the three of them stood quietly for a moment, the reality of their task settling back in. They all knew the Dogman was still out there, somewhere in the shadows. And when it came back, they'd be ready—even if Sheriff Becan wasn't.

Beretti glanced at Jacobi and Perry. "We're not done for the night yet. Let's swing by Eunice's place on our way to do the rounds around town, make sure he went home and isn't out stirring up more trouble. You remember where that is, right, Jacobi?" she added with a smirk.

Jacobi straightened, tossing his empty coffee cup into the back of the SUV. "Yes, Beretti, I remember," he said, chuckling a bit sheepishly.

As they climbed into their vehicles, a light rain began to fall, misting the windshields and adding a damp chill to the night. Perry sighed, looking already worn down. "I'll keep looping around town. Let's just hope he's not out starting another riot."

With that, they drove off into the wet, darkened streets.

FORTY-THREE

Perry navigated the quiet streets, scanning for any lingering vigilantes who might still be wandering around, looking for trouble, as well as any sign of the Dogman. The town had gone eerily still in the early hours, save for the occasional house with lights still on. His eyes were growing heavy when his phone vibrated. Deputy Signe.

"Hey, boss, I looked into Chuck Pantanie for you," Signe's voice came through, steady but with a hint of urgency. "It's…interesting. We'll need a warrant for his bank records, but I think he's worth a closer look."

"Go on," Perry replied, his curiosity piqued.

"Seems Chucky boy has a history of trouble with wildlife

laws. He was busted in California for illegally hunting mountain lions a few years back, and there are warrants out for him in South Dakota for similar offenses. Also, his neighbor claims his house is covered in hides—deer, bear, mountain lion, even wolf mounts. He's got a real setup."

Perry's eyes narrowed. "So, Pantanie could be running a whole illegal trapping ring out here, supplying hides and mounts, maybe even to buyers out of state?"

"Wouldn't surprise me. This guy's been deep in it for a long time," Signe replied.

"Thanks for looking into it," Perry said, ending the call. Pocketing his phone, he couldn't shake the feeling that Chuck Pantanie might be the one Tucker had gotten in too deep with.

FORTY-FOUR

The roads were quiet, with only the gentle rhythm of the tires on wet pavement filling the silence. Beretti leaned back in her seat, her gaze shifting between the windshield and the side mirror, the steady sweep of the wipers almost hypnotic against the light drizzle outside. Jacobi, hands firm on the wheel, finally broke the silence.

"So, what do you think the sheriff was up to tonight, showing up like that?" Jacobi asked, his voice casual but curious.

Beretti chuckled lightly, her lips curling into a slight smirk. "Who knows? Probably being pressured by the Mayor. You know how politics works—keep up appearances and all that." She glanced out the window, watching the trees pass by in a blur of motion. "Could be that the Mayor wants him out in the open a bit more, trying to look like he's doing something. But honestly, I'm not buying it."

Jacobi nodded, his fingers tapping on the steering wheel. "Yeah, that makes sense. The sheriff's barely done a thing since we got here, and now he's trying to act like he's been running the show."

"Exactly," Beretti agreed, shaking her head. "It's all a performance. The town's falling apart, and all Becan can think about is his reputation. Meanwhile, the real danger is out here."

Jacobi shot her a sidelong glance. "You think the Mayor's giving him heat for not handling it better?"

"Absolutely," she said without hesitation. "A few more attacks like tonight, and people are going to start asking for the sheriff to resign. The Mayor won't want that heat on his own doorstep, particularly as it's his brother-in-law, so he'll push Becan to make it look like they're on top of things." She sighed. "But we know who's really handling it."

Jacobi chuckled, shaking his head. "Yeah, us and Perry."

They drove on in silence, the quiet stretching as they

approached Eunice's neighborhood. Beretti leaned forward, her gaze sharpening as something caught her eye.

"Well, that's not good," she muttered, her tone uneasy.

About 500 yards from Eunice's house, his pickup truck lay abandoned in a ditch. Jacobi slowed, casting a quick glance at the empty truck before continuing to up the road.

The SUV slowed as they neared Eunice's house, its headlights cutting through the dark. Jacobi narrowed his eyes, noticing something off in the distance. The front yard was the same disheveled mess it always was, but there was something else—something wrong.

"Ahhh man," Jacobi muttered, easing his foot off the gas.

Beretti leaned forward, her gaze locking onto the house. The front door was missing. Gone.

"This is bad," she murmured, while already grabbing her phone. Her instincts kicked in, and without hesitation, she dialed Chief Deputy Perry.

The SUV rolled to a stop a few feet from the driveway, both agents exchanging a grim look. Jacobi clicked the engine off, the quiet settling over them like a thick blanket. Neither of them liked the way this looked.

"Perry," Beretti said when he answered. "We're out the front of Eunice's place. The front door's gone. Completely ripped off. We were going to check inside, but I thought I'd call you first."

There was a pause on the other end before Perry's voice came through, firm and tense. "Don't go in. I'll be there in eight minutes—wait for me before you head inside. It could be dangerous."

Beretti's eyes flicked to Jacobi, who had already unholstered his weapon, his flashlight trained on the house. "Got it. We'll wait here," she replied and hung up the phone.

Jacobi exhaled slowly, still staring at the darkened house. "Eight minutes," he said, stepping out of the SUV but keeping his distance from the house. Beretti followed, standing next to him, her hand resting lightly on her sidearm.

They didn't venture any closer to the house. Instead, they stayed by the SUV, both agents scanning the area, listening for any signs of movement. The air was cold and still, the tension tangible.

While Beretti kept an eye out, Jacobi opened the trunk and grabbed two of their high-powered rifles out of the back and passed one to Beretti.

After checking their rifles were ready and loaded, they stood in silence, alert and waiting, the haunting quiet of the night surrounding them as they kept their eyes trained on the house and surrounding area, knowing something wasn't right.

FORTY-FIVE

The rumble of Perry's cruiser broke the quiet that hung in the air around Eunice's house. Beretti and Jacobi waited by the SUV, watching as Perry stepped out, his face a mix of concern and determination. He didn't waste any time, joining them with his flashlight ready.

"Let's make this quick," Perry said, his voice low but tense as he grabbed his shotgun. He glanced at the missing door and the darkened house beyond. "Well, that doesn't look promising."

Beretti nodded, taking the lead as she pulled out her flashlight. "We'll go in together," she said. Jacobi followed closely, his head on a swivel as they moved toward the house.

As they approached the front porch, the house, with its missing door and gaping entrance, looked even more foreboding in the dim light. The air smelled of decay and something far more sinister.

Just as they were about to step onto the porch, a sharp rustling came from the bushes to their right.

All three froze.

Their flashlights swung toward the sound, beams of light slicing through the darkness. The noise continued—rustling, like something moving through the underbrush. Beretti's heart pounded in her chest, her grip on her weapon tightening.

Perry's breath hitched, and Jacobi tensed, every muscle coiled as they waited for whatever was lurking to emerge. The night was eerily quiet, as if everything was frozen in time.

Then, after what felt like an eternity, something darted out of the bushes.

A raccoon.

It scurried across the yard, chasing after a mouse, its small body disappearing back into the shrubs almost as quickly as it had appeared.

The three of them exhaled in unison, tension draining from their bodies.

"Damn raccoon," Jacobi muttered, shaking his head. "At least it wasn't the Dogman." He cracked a grin, trying to break the lingering tension. "Looks like even the wildlife is in on the horror show tonight."

Beretti smirked, her pulse slowly returning to normal. "Let's just hope the next thing we see isn't a lot bigger."

Perry chuckled softly, though his eyes remained fixed on the house. "Hopefully not."

The moment of relief passed, and the three resumed their slow approach, walking up the creaky porch steps. Every sound was amplified—the creak of the wood beneath their feet, and their own breaths coming in measured, steady rhythms. The night felt alive with tension, as if something was watching them from the darkness.

Inside, the air was thick with the metallic scent of blood. Beretti's flashlight scanned the room, revealing overturned furniture and deep gouges in the floor. And then, in the far corner, they saw it—Eunice's body, crumpled and torn apart.

"Jesus," Jacobi whispered, his voice tight. "Where's his face?"

Beretti crouched, examining the shredded remains. "It fed on him," she confirmed.

Perry's face twisted with disgust as he stood back. "Why Eunice? Why would the Dogman go after him?"

Beretti stood, wiping a hand across her face. "Eunice shot at it. Dogmen can be very revengeful. It probably picked up his scent and tracked him home. Once they feel threatened, they don't let it go."

Jacobi added, "This wasn't just an attack—it was personal. Eunice was marked."

Perry sighed deeply, pulling out his phone. "I'll call the coroner and another deputy to lock this down."

Minutes later, the crunch of tires on gravel announced the arrival of the young deputy. He stepped out with a look of determined focus, eager to show Perry what he was capable of. As he approached the house, he squared his shoulders, a flicker of pride in his eyes. But the moment he stepped inside, that confidence shattered.

He took one look at Eunice's remains, his face draining of color. Turning on his heel, he barely made it outside before doubling over, retching into the bushes.

Perry shook his head. "He'll get used it. We all do."

Right when things were starting to quiet down, the sudden noise of a car screeching into the driveway shattered the silence once again. A beat-up sedan jerked to a stop, and the door flew open. Eunice's girlfriend, looking frazzled and smelling of cheap perfume and cigarettes, stormed out of the car.

She marched toward them, her heels clicking on the pavement, her voice sharp and angry before she even reached them. "What the hell's going on here? What'd you do to Eunice?!"

Perry stepped forward, raising his hands in an attempt to calm her. "Ma'am, this is a crime scene, and I'm sorry to tell you that Eunice has been killed."

The words hung in the air, and for a moment, she froze. "Killed?" she repeated, blinking as if trying to process what she'd just heard. Her eyes darted between Perry and the house. "No... no, you're lying! Eunice ain't dead!" Her voice grew shrill, her denial twisting into something more volatile.

"Ma'am," Perry said calmly, "I'm afraid it's true. Eunice was—"

"Don't you tell me that!" she shrieked, cutting him off.

"This is your fault! Did you shoot him?" Her voice was raw with accusation, and she pointed an angry finger at the officers. "You pigs did this! I knew it!"

The fury in her voice seemed to shake the air. She pushed past Perry, her eyes wild. "I'm going inside!" she demanded.

The young deputy stepped in front of her, raising his hands. "Ma'am, you can't go in there. It's a crime scene."

She sneered, leaning in close enough to make him flinch. "Your breath smells like shit," she barked, her painted-on eyebrows knitting together in fury. "And I don't care who says I can't be here! Eunice is my man—you don't get to tell me what to do!"

She shoved at him, but the deputy held his ground, glancing nervously at Perry, who stepped forward to defuse the situation.

"You can't go in, ma'am," Perry said firmly, though his voice wavered slightly.

Her glare sharpened, her face twisting with rage. "This is all your fault! You let this happen! And now you won't even let me see him?! What kind of monsters are you?"

Beretti stepped forward, her voice calm but commanding.

"We didn't do this. We're trying to help. But right now, you need to step back."

The woman's eyes narrowed at Beretti, fury overtaking reason as she swung a hand to strike her. But Beretti reacted quickly, catching the woman's arm mid-swing and firmly pushing her back. She stumbled, losing her balance and falling onto the ground, landing hard on her rear.

Perry stepped forward, his voice cold and unyielding. "Get out of here before I arrest you for obstruction. Last warning."

The woman shot him a venomous glare, but something in Perry's tone made her think twice. Muttering under her breath, she got to her feet and backed away, throwing a final glare at the officers before retreating down the driveway.

"I'll see y'all in hell for this," she spat, before getting back in her car. "This ain't over!"

She slammed the door and peeled out of the driveway, the screech of tires cutting through the night as she disappeared into the dark.

Jacobi watched her tail lights fade, then glanced at the young deputy, who looked rattled and slightly green around the gills.

"Here, kid," Jacobi said, digging into his pocket and handing over a mint with a sympathetic smirk. "Might help."

The deputy flushed, mumbling a quiet thanks as he accepted the mint, and Jacobi couldn't help but chuckle under his breath.

Perry let out a long sigh, rubbing his temples. "Well, that went about as well as I expected."

Jacobi shook his head, still watching the dust settle. "She's gonna be a real problem."

Beretti crossed her arms, eyes still fixed on the road. "We've got bigger problems to handle right now."

FORTY-SIX

Early the next morning, Beretti and Jacobi sat at a small diner on the edge of town, sipping their coffee as the sunlight began to creep over the horizon. They hadn't come across anything else during their rounds last night, and there had been no new attacks after what happened to Eunice. Though the quiet was almost a relief, it also meant the Dogman was still out there, lurking, waiting to strike again. The sense of unease lingered.

Beretti stirred her coffee absently, her mind already racing through different scenarios. "We need a clearer plan," she said, her voice firm but low. "This thing is smart. It's picking its moments. We can't keep reacting after the fact, or more people are going to get killed."

She raised an eyebrow and tried again. "Jacobi?"

He looked up, blinking as if snapped from a trance. "Sorry, what was that? Got distracted by the local FB page. It's worse than ever—people are scared and mad. And look at this."

He handed her the phone, showing the latest posts on the town's forum. The feed was flooded with rumors, accusations, and a growing number of posts demanding action, or even suggesting more people take things into their own hands. Beretti's gaze narrowed as she scanned through, her expression darkening when she reached the posts from Eunice's girlfriend, Amber.

"She's been at it all night," Jacobi muttered, his thumb swiping down to reveal a long thread of unhinged comments. "Amber's posting about a conspiracy between us and the sheriff's department. She's claiming the Dogman didn't kill Eunice, that we set him up to be killed by the creature."

Beretti leaned in, scanning the screen. "Well, that is creative of her."

Jacobi nodded. "She's got a few supporters, but most people are calling her crazy. Some of her posts have been deleted by the forum mods, but she keeps going. She's even posting it all on her personal page now, throwing out more hate."

Beretti let out a slow breath. "She's grieving in her own way, but this... this could become a problem if more people start believing her."

"She's already painted a target on our backs," Jacobi added. "And it doesn't help that the sheriff isn't exactly a *beacon* of trust in this town."

Beretti gave a dry laugh. "I see what you did there. I agree with you. Sheriff Becan isn't doing us any favors." She took a sip of her coffee and glanced out the window at the quiet street. "The last thing we need is a mob believing that we're somehow in league with the Dogman."

Jacobi nodded, scrolling through more comments. "Luckily, most people are shutting her down, calling her out, but she's persistent. She's up all night, throwing out accusations. It's only a matter of time before she escalates."

Beretti set down her cup and pulled out her phone, dialing ASAC Ward. She needed to update him on the situation before things spiraled further.

The phone rang twice before Ward's voice came through, calm and direct. "Beretti. Give me an update."

"We're still hunting the Dogman," Beretti began, leaning back in her seat. "Last night was quiet. No new attacks since Eunice, but his girlfriend, Amber, has been stirring things up online. She's claiming there's a conspiracy between us and the sheriff's department, saying we set Eunice up to be killed."

Ward sighed on the other end of the line. "I've seen this before. People lash out when they can't handle the truth. Do you need more resources? Backup?"

"No," Beretti said confidently, glancing at Jacobi, who was still scrolling through his phone. "The two of us can handle this. But it's getting complicated. We're dealing with more than just the creature now—we've got townspeople on edge, and Amber's making things worse."

There was a pause before Ward responded. "Alright. I trust your judgment. Just be careful. This kind of public paranoia can get dangerous fast."

"Understood," Beretti replied. She hesitated, then added, "Any updates on the… other thing?"

Ward's tone shifted slightly, more serious. "Not yet. They're digging, but still need a little time. I'll keep you posted."

"Appreciate it," Beretti said. "I'll keep you updated here."

"Good luck," Ward added before the line clicked off.

Jacobi looked up from his phone, nodding in agreement. "So, what's the next move?"

Beretti thought for a moment, then leaned forward. "We walk the streets tonight. No more driving around in the SUV. This thing is smart, it knows we're hunting it, and it's staying just out of reach. We need to change the game. We need to make ourselves bait, draw it out."

Jacobi raised an eyebrow. "You want us to walk around town, hoping the Dogman comes after us?"

Beretti smiled grimly. "It's a risk, but it might be the only way to get it to show itself. We're not going to catch it by driving around in circles. We need to make it think we're vulnerable, like easy prey."

Jacobi leaned back in his chair, a half-smile tugging at the corner of his mouth. "Sounds like one of my crazy plans. I knew there was a reason I liked working with you—always thinking outside the box."

Beretti chuckled, though there was little humor in it. "Maybe so, but we're going out there as a team, not alone. It's either that or wait for the next body to turn up, and I'm not doing that."

Jacobi nodded, his expression serious. "Agreed. Let's get this done together."

Beretti nodded. "We'll gear up and hit the streets tonight. If we can draw it out, we end this before more people get hurt."

The two of them finished their coffee, the unspoken anticipation hanging in the air between them. Tonight was going to be different. They weren't just hunting the Dogman anymore—they were going to put themselves in its path, hoping to end the nightmare before it spiraled further out of control.

As they stood to leave, Beretti glanced at Jacobi. "Try and get some rest when we get back to the hotel. No sneaking out. Tonight, we're going to need all the energy we can get."

Jacobi smirked. "Rest? After everything we've seen? I'll try, but don't hold your breath."

Beretti shook her head, already mentally preparing for the long night ahead. They had a plan now. And with any luck, it would be their last night on this hunt.

FORTY-SEVEN

Jacobi and Beretti stepped out of the small-town diner, letting the door swing shut behind them as the chill morning air greeted them. They'd spent breakfast hashing out plans, but both knew the town's problems were far from solved.

Jacobi stretched, rubbing his lower back with a faint grimace. "Either those diner chairs are getting harder, or I'm getting too old for this," he muttered, smirking at Beretti.

Beretti gave him a dry smile, her gaze already scanning the empty parking lot. "Agreed. At 29, you're practically due for retirement."

Jacobi chuckled. "Yeah, yeah, alright."

They were almost at the SUV when they heard footsteps behind them and a voice call out. "Hey! Wait!"

Jacobi turned, spotting Amber—Eunice's girlfriend—striding toward them. Her eyes were red and puffy, like she'd been up all night. He immediately tensed, the feeling in his gut saying this wasn't going to be good.

Amber slowed as she reached them, her hands raised in a gesture of surrender. "I just want to talk," she said, her voice trembling.

Jacobi shared a quick look with Beretti before stepping forward with a skeptical grin. "What's up, Amber?"

Amber blinked up at him, her eyes big and watery. "I—I've been a mess," she stammered. "All the things I posted online, the hate... I didn't mean it. I was just angry, grieving. You know how that is, right?" She looked at Jacobi with wide eyes, wringing her hands nervously. "I'm sorry."

Jacobi let his gaze linger on her for a moment, unimpressed. "Sure, Amber. But you've gotta be careful what you throw out there. People believe that garbage. You're stirring up a mess you can't control."

Amber nodded, taking a small step closer, her gaze darting between him and Beretti. "I know, I know. That's why

I wanted to talk to you." She reached out tentatively, almost as if she wanted to touch his arm, her voice dropping into a softer tone. "Could we maybe... talk? Alone?"

Beretti watched, her brow furrowing, but stayed back, giving Jacobi space. Jacobi knew better than to fall for Amber's act, but he was curious enough to see what she was trying to pull.

"Alright, let's hear it," he said, glancing back at Beretti with a wink. "But let's keep this quick."

He took a few steps closer to Amber, just outside Beretti's reach. Amber's lips curled into a coy smile. "Thanks... you're kinder than I expected. I really appreciate it."

Before he could reply, a huge figure lunged from behind a parked car—a massive man, easily over six feet tall and built like a mountain. Jacobi barely had time to brace himself before a fist collided with his ribs. The blow knocked the wind out of him, sending him stumbling back into the SUV.

Jacobi managed a strained laugh, catching his breath. "Wow, Amber, you got yourself a new boyfriend already?" he asked, wincing.

The brute took another swing, aiming for his face. Jacobi ducked, twisting away and letting the fist sail past him.

"Almost got me," he taunted, giving the guy a quick, sarcastic salute as he rolled along the car's side.

Amber cackled, her voice shrill. "Fuck him up Ray! Show the fuckin' pig who runs this town!"

Jacobi barely had time to quip back before the brute grabbed him by the collar, slamming him against the SUV hard enough to rattle the windows. Jacobi grunted but kept his smirk intact. "Really? That's your best?" he asked, struggling against the man's grip.

Seeing the attack unfold, Beretti unholstered her gun, but was unable to fire with Jacobi in the middle of it. She darted toward them, barking, "Get off him!"

The man ignored her, reeling his fist back for another punch. But Jacobi twisted away at the last second, sending them both sprawling to the ground in a tangle of fists and elbows.

Beretti closed the distance, sizing up the brute's massive frame. He was strong, but she'd brought down bigger. Jacobi was holding his own, but the man's bulk was wearing him down. As the brute pressed Jacobi to the ground, Beretti moved in with precision, locking her grip around his arm and twisting it sharply. She followed up with a swift hip throw, sending him crashing onto the dirt.

Amber's grin vanished as she watched her accomplice get taken down. She took a step back, eyes wide.

The brute struggled to rise, but Beretti wasn't letting up. She dropped her knee onto his chest, pinning him to the ground while twisting his wrist into a submission hold. "Move, and I'll snap it," she said coldly. The man let out a low groan, knowing he was beaten.

Jacobi staggered to his feet, dusting himself off with a pained grin. "Didn't even break a sweat," he said, catching his breath. "Nice move, though."

Beretti didn't miss a beat, snapping two sets of cuffs on the guy's wrists before helping Jacobi stand. "You okay?" she asked, her voice tinged with mild amusement.

Jacobi wiped a smear of blood from his lip, wincing. "Oh, you know. Just wasn't expecting breakfast with a side of sucker punch." He raised an eyebrow. "Though next time, you can let me handle it. I had him right where I wanted him."

Beretti rolled her eyes. "Sure you did." She called in the incident, and five minutes later, a deputy arrived to haul the man off to the station.

Meanwhile, Beretti turned to Amber, her gaze steely. "Get out of here before I decide to arrest you too."

Amber hesitated, scowling, but the look in Beretti's eyes told her she'd pushed her luck. With a final glare, she stomped off, muttering under her breath.

Once she was gone, Beretti looked back at Jacobi with a smirk. "You good?"

Jacobi nodded, still catching his breath. "Yeah. Guess my charm's a magnet for trouble."

Beretti chuckled. "Might be worth turning down the charm next time. People like Amber are getting desperate."

Jacobi's grin returned, cocky as ever. "Desperate people are my specialty."

FORTY-EIGHT

Sheriff Becan pulled up in front of the Mayor's house, already irritated. The Mayor was hiding out, of course. The town was in an uproar, people demanding answers, but Ed—the Mayor—had retreated into his cushy home, away from the chaos.

As Becan climbed out of his cruiser, he muttered under his breath, already knowing this wasn't going to be a pleasant conversation. He straightened his shirt, though it was still wrinkled and his appearance far from sharp. He didn't care anymore.

He knocked on the door, not bothering to wait for long before it swung open. Mayor Ed Ralston stood there, his face ashen, eyes darting nervously.

"What are you doing here, Becan?" the Mayor hissed, glancing over his shoulder as though expecting someone to jump out from the shadows. "I told you to handle this! The town is going crazy, and they're looking to me for answers I don't have!"

"I'm handling it," Becan growled, stepping inside without waiting for an invitation. "Where do you think I've been all morning? Talking people down, dealing with the FBI. But here you are, hiding in your nice house while the rest of us are out there taking the heat."

The Mayor scowled, leading the sheriff into the living room. The curtains were drawn, the room dim despite the bright morning sun outside. It was clear the Mayor hadn't left the house in days, avoiding any confrontation with the furious townspeople. The contrast between the pristine home and the chaos outside was almost laughable.

"I'm not hiding," the Mayor snapped, though the nervous look in his eyes said otherwise. "I'm staying out of sight until you get a handle on this thing. Now tell me, what's your plan? What are you doing to catch this creature?"

Becan wandered over to the Mayor's liquor cabinet,

casually pouring himself a drink before settling into one of the overstuffed chairs with a sigh. "The Feds are handling it," he said nonchalantly, waving his hand as he took a sip. "They're the ones out there hunting the creature. When they catch it—or kill it—I'll take the credit for keeping the town safe."

Ed's face tightened with frustration. "You think it'll be that simple? Just sit back and let them do the hard work, and then swoop in for the glory?"

Becan shrugged. "It's worked before."

The Mayor wasn't having it. "This isn't like before. The town's in a panic, and people are looking to you for leadership. They don't trust you, Becan, and they certainly won't just accept you taking credit. You've been too lazy, too absent."

"Lazy?" Becan's face darkened. "I've been doing everything I can to keep people calm. You think I want to be in the middle of this mess? The Feds are the ones trained for this kind of thing. Let them handle it."

The Mayor scoffed, refusing to back down. "You're delusional, Becan. Did you know Maureen was accosted in the Dillard's parking lot yesterday, and she came home in tears? I had to send her to her sisters to wait this out safely."

Becan snorted, rolling his eyes. "Yeah, well, Maureen always was a wuss. Just like her husband, hiding from his own town instead of facing it."

The Mayor's face flushed, fists clenching. "You're a real piece of work, Becan. This town deserves more than a sheriff who's all talk and no action."

"Then go out there and see what you can handle yourself Ed!" Becan snapped back. "But until you do, keep that mouth shut and let me do my damn job."

"The only reason you have kept your job this long is because of me, Donald. It's probably about time you stepped down."

Becan's fists clenched, his anger flaring. "Step down? You have no idea what it takes to do my job," he shot back.

The Mayor didn't flinch, his eyes narrowing with defiance. "You think I'm afraid of you, Becan? Of what you know?" He leaned closer, his tone sharp. "I can find someone who knows how to keep things under control without the constant mess. Maybe someone with loyalty."

For a brief second, Becan's face fell, but he quickly regained his bravado. "When this is over, I'll handle it. Just like I always do."

Ed's expression didn't soften. "You say that, but if this goes south, don't expect me to cover for you again."

The room was filled with a tense silence, as the impact of their argument was clearly felt. Becan's blood was boiling, but he knew pushing it further wasn't going to get him anywhere. He was done here.

"Keep hiding in your house, Mayor," Becan sneered, heading toward the door. "I've got a town to take care of."

Without waiting for a response, he stormed out of the house, slamming the door behind him. His mind was racing, anger bubbling up inside. He had no intention of letting the Mayor or anyone else question his authority again.

FORTY-NINE

The late afternoon light filtered softly through the curtains as Beretti stirred. Stretching with a sigh, she swung her legs over the side of the bed and headed straight for the shower. The hot water was a relief, easing the stress as she closed her eyes and let herself relax, even just for a minute. Afterward, she dressed, slipping into her tactical gear, her mind already focused on the plan for the night ahead.

She double-checked the pouches on her belt and vest, then reached for her trusty KA-BAR knife, securing it in place. With one last sweep over her gear, she glanced at her firearms on the desk, each one freshly cleaned and ready.

Before touching them, she reached for her phone and dialed Perry. The line rang twice before his now familiar voice answered.

"Beretti," Perry greeted her. His tone was calm but carried the weight of the ongoing chaos.

"Evening, Perry," Beretti replied, leaning against the desk. "Just checking in. Jacobi and I have a plan for tonight. We're going to be walking the streets, seeing if we can stir something up and keep an eye on the situation."

Perry let out a short chuckle. "Stir something up, huh? Well, I'll be out patrolling with Deputy Delvaney tonight. You give me a call if you need any backup, alright?"

"You got it," she responded, grateful for his support. "Thanks, Perry."

"Be safe out there," Perry added before hanging up.

Beretti slid her phone back into her pocket just as Jacobi came through the door. He was already dressed and geared up, his rifle slung over his shoulder and his sidearm holstered at his hip.

"I'm ready when you are," Jacobi said, flashing a grin that didn't quite reach his eyes. Despite his calm demeanor, the weight of the night ahead was evident in the tension lining his face.

Beretti gave a small nod, then turned to check her own firearms. Her fingers moved skillfully, examining her high-powered rifle that was armed with armor-piercing rounds—an essential requirement for hunting cryptids. Next, she checked her .40 cal S&W pistol, making sure it was locked, loaded, and ready. Securing the weapon at her side, she found comfort in its familiar weight.

"Good to go," Beretti confirmed, glancing at Jacobi.

"Same here," he replied, adjusting the strap on his rifle. "This is going to be one hell of a night, isn't it?"

Beretti smirked. "Sure feels like it."

A light rain was falling as they made their way to a small convenience store near the edge of town. They knew they had a few hours before the real hunt began, but neither of them wanted to be caught unprepared. "Let's grab something to eat before things get wild," Beretti suggested.

Jacobi agreed, and they walked into the quiet store, where the smell of fresh coffee mingled with the scent of dust and aging shelves. They grabbed a couple of pre-packaged sandwiches from the cooler and poured themselves large coffees, the steam curling up in the cozy store.

The old man behind the counter gave them a friendly nod. "Y'all have a safe night, officers."

As they made their way to the SUV, one of the men standing by the pickup truck whistled, catching the attention of his friends. "Hey, sweetheart!" he called, his voice thick with condescension. "You're too pretty to be an FBI agent. Why don't you come over here and show us what you're really good at?"

Jacobi's grip on his coffee cup tightened, his shoulders tensing, but Beretti cut him off with a quick, cool glance. "Don't. Stay focused and ignore them."

The men continued their jeering as Beretti and Jacobi approached the SUV, their laughter ringing through the lot.

As they got into the SUV and drove off, Jacobi shook his head, glancing at Beretti. "How do you put up with that kind of crap? All that whistling and the comments—don't you ever want to let them have it?"

Beretti kept her eyes on the road ahead, her expression unbothered. "I ignore it unless they cross the line," she replied calmly.

Jacobi raised an eyebrow. "And then?"

Her mouth curled into a slight smile. "Then I show them just how fast I can take them down."

FIFTY

The rain had slowed to a steady drizzle by the time Beretti and Jacobi found themselves walking the quiet streets of the small town. Thunder rumbled faintly in the distance as they patrolled, side by side, their boots splashing through puddles as they scanned the streets for any sign of the Dogman.

"So, I've never actually asked you this. How long have you been doing this?" Jacobi queried, breaking the silence as they passed the corner of a hardware store.

"Long enough," Beretti replied, her eyes scanning dark alleyways and dimly lit windows for any movement.

Jacobi chuckled. "That's vague. Starting to get the feeling

you're a woman of few words, Beretti."

She smirked. "Only when the job calls for it."

Jacobi shrugged, looking ahead. "Fair enough. Ever had a husband?"

Beretti's expression remained steady, though her eyes shifted slightly with a brief hesitation before she answered. "No. Relationships in this line of work... they're complicated."

Jacobi nodded, intrigued but careful not to push. "Yeah, I get that. I had a few relationships tank because of the job. They either couldn't handle the long hours or figured I was traveling to see other women."

Beretti gave a small smile but didn't respond, letting silence settle between them. Jacobi, however, wasn't done. "So, was there ever anyone special?"

For a moment, she didn't answer, her gaze fixed straight ahead, scanning the darkened streets. "Yes," she said finally, her voice quieter. "A long time ago."

Jacobi raised an eyebrow. "What happened?"

Beretti paused, then shot him a sidelong glance. "The usual. But right now we've got more important things to worry about." Her tone signaled that the conversation was over, and Jacobi took the hint.

Aside from the occasional car, the town was deserted. The sheriff hadn't ordered a curfew, but the townsfolk had taken their own precautions, staying inside. After a few more minutes, Beretti slowed, stopping near an abandoned house.

"I've been thinking," she said, her voice low and serious. "We've been walking together for hours, and nothing. This thing is smart; it's probably watching us, waiting for the right moment to strike."

Jacobi turned to her, frowning. "You want to split up, don't you?"

She nodded. "Yes. We split up, make it look like you're alone. That'll make you more vulnerable, hopefully drawing the Dogman out. I'll flank you from the shadows, keep you in my sights the whole time."

Jacobi crossed his arms, considering the plan. "So, I'm the bait. You really think it'll work?"

Beretti nodded firmly. "I do. Right now, we're just wandering, hoping to stumble into it. This way, we control the encounter."

Jacobi sighed, running a hand through his damp hair. "Alright. Let's do it. But if you see it coming, don't wait—take the shot."

"Don't worry, I'll be ready," she said confidently.

They stood for a moment before parting ways. Jacobi knew this was a risky move, but he trusted Beretti. She hadn't let him down yet.

"Alright," Jacobi said, exhaling deeply. "I'll keep walking. You stay behind me. We keep in contact through the earpiece."

"Exactly," Beretti agreed, already fading into the shadows of a nearby alley. "Stay safe, Jacobi. I'll be right behind you."

Jacobi nodded and set off down the street alone, the steady rhythm of his footsteps the only sound breaking the quiet night. His heart rate picked up slightly, knowing Beretti was no longer at his side. He was walking into a trap—a trap they'd set themselves. But that didn't make it any less nerve-wracking.

"Can you hear me?" Jacobi asked quietly, tapping his earpiece.

"Loud and clear," Beretti's voice responded, crackling slightly in his ear.

As he walked, his gaze swept over each alley and yard, alert and watchful. The town felt abandoned, but he knew better. The Dogman was out there, lurking, waiting for the perfect moment. If it felt safe venturing into town last night, it would again tonight.

The minutes dragged on, the anxiety in Jacobi's stomach growing with every step. His hands tightened around the grip of his rifle, his senses heightened as he moved deeper into town. The rain had tapered off, but the streets were still slick, the wet asphalt reflecting the dim glow of the streetlights.

"How's it looking back there?" Jacobi asked, trying to keep his voice steady.

"I've got you in my sights," Beretti replied, her tone calm. "Nothing yet. Keep walking."

Jacobi nodded to himself, his breath coming in shallow bursts as he continued forward. The quiet was unnerving. Every sound, every shift in the wind, felt like a potential threat. The Dogman was smart, maybe even smarter than they'd given it credit for. It wouldn't strike unless it thought it had the advantage.

FIFTY-ONE

Jacobi continued his patrol down the deserted streets, each step feeling heavier as adrenaline coursed through him. They had been at this for twenty minutes, and his senses were on high alert. The plan was simple: make Jacobi appear vulnerable and alone while Beretti flanked him from a distance, hidden in the dark. The Dogman had to believe he was an easy target. And when it finally came for him, they would be ready.

The rain was still falling, dripping down Jacobi's face as he wiped it away, his shoulders tense. Every now and then, he'd glance around, reassured by the knowledge that Beretti had his back—even if he couldn't see her.

The streets were quiet, too quiet, and both agents knew what that meant: the Dogman was out there, waiting for the right moment.

Suddenly, headlights illuminated Jacobi from behind. The engine's low hum broke the silence of the night as a patrol car slowly pulled up next to him.

Deputy Perry.

Jacobi slowed, a bit of relief crossing his face as the car window rolled down.

"Jacobi," Perry called out, frowning in confusion. "What the hell are you doing out here alone?"

"We're running a plan," Jacobi replied. "Beretti's in the shadows, flanking me. We're trying to lure it out."

Perry glanced around, suspicion still on his face, though he trusted the agents. "You sure this is a good idea?"

"It's the best idea we have right now. We need to draw it out before it kills someone else."

Perry grunted in acknowledgment. "Alright. Just... be careful. I'll keep an eye out."

Beretti stayed crouched behind a row of bushes, watching

the exchange, her hand ready on her weapon in case the Dogman took the opportunity to attack. She remained still as Perry drove off, casting one last worried glance at Jacobi.

Once Perry's car disappeared into the night, Jacobi continued walking, his heart racing but his pace steady. Beretti followed from her position, cutting through front yards and weaving between trees and houses to keep a low profile.

As Jacobi passed an alley, he crossed the street, moving slowly, his eyes darting left and right.

Beretti followed a safe distance behind, her focus wavering between his back and the street.

As she neared the alley, her boot landed on glass with a sharp, unmistakable crunch. She stood still, heart racing, looking straight ahead.

Jacobi froze as the sound of breaking glass pierced through the stillness, his head snapping around. He saw Beretti's boot slip on a shard, her stance tensing just before his gaze shifted to something far more unsettling—two amber eyes gleaming from deep within the alley. Fierce and focused entirely on Beretti. From where she stood, she couldn't see it.

In an instant, the Dogman rose from the darkness, its

massive body coiling, muscles rippling beneath its thick, dark fur.

"Beretti, run!" Jacobi bellowed, his voice loud and sharp. Without hesitation, she bolted back the way they'd come, her footsteps echoing. Jacobi raised his rifle and fired, the shot slicing through the darkness and grazing the creature's shoulder. The Dogman recoiled but didn't fall. He fired again, aiming lower, the bullet striking close to its leg. The creature hesitated, its lips pulling back in a furious snarl, but as Beretti's scent faded, its gaze snapped back toward her path, driven by instinct to chase.

Beretti bolted, her heart hammering as she sprinted down the street. Her breaths came fast and shallow as she veered between two houses, hoping to throw it off her trail. Spotting a fence up ahead, she gathered herself and leapt. Pain shot through her arm as it snagged on a jagged piece of metal, slicing deep. Gritting her teeth, she yanked herself free, feeling warm blood trickle down as she hit the ground on the other side.

Gasping, she scanned the street and saw it—the vacant house they'd passed earlier, with a faded FOR SALE sign swaying in the breeze. She sprinted up the steps, threw the door open, and darted inside, slamming it shut behind her.

She moved quickly through the darkened living room and slipped into the kitchen, lowering herself onto the cold tile floor. Lying flat on her stomach, she ignored the throbbing in her injured arm as she gripped her rifle, aiming it toward the front door.

Jacobi chased after the Dogman as it weaved down the street, dodging his shots with unnerving agility. Up ahead, he saw Beretti vault the fence and disappear into the house. The Dogman didn't even break stride, clearing the fence with a single, powerful leap as it closed in on her.

Jacobi sprinted harder, desperation pushing him forward. The creature was fast—too fast. As it bounded up onto the porch, Jacobi fired another shot, aiming to draw its attention. The shot echoed through the night, causing the Dogman to pause, its amber eyes flicking back in his direction. But it quickly turned, refocusing on the front door.

Jacobi rushed across the road, dodging a passing car, and yelling, "Move!" as he crossed behind it.

Inside, Beretti lay flat on the cold kitchen tiles, her breath shallow as she gripped her rifle, ears tuned to the silence. The room was dark, lit only by a faint glow from the streetlamp outside, as she braced herself for what was coming.

She heard it—the scrape of claws on wood, the Dogman's guttural breaths as it sniffed, tracking her scent to the door. Each heavy step pressed through the silence, growing louder. Beretti took a shallow breath, forcing herself to ignore the pain in her arm, her gaze locked on the doorway.

Then, with a powerful crash, the front door splintered, and the Dogman's massive form filled the entryway. Its amber eyes scanned the room, locking onto her in the dim light. For a moment, she froze. Its gaze narrowed, lips pulling back in a grimace as it crouched to lunge, claws extended.

"Come on, you bastard," she whispered, voice barely audible. Steeling herself, she squeezed the trigger.

The rifle roared, and the bullet struck the Dogman's jaw, snapping its head sideways. The creature staggered, releasing a garbled, blood-choked growl, pain blazing in its eyes as it fought to stay upright.

Beretti braced herself, tightened her grip, and squeezed the trigger again. The shot rang out, striking just above the creature's eyes. The Dogman trembled, swayed, and then fell to the ground with a loud thud, remaining motionless.

Silence settled once more, thick and absolute. Still lying flat, Beretti allowed herself a deep breath, the rifle resting limply against the floor as the reality of what had just happened set in.

FIFTY-TWO

Jacobi's heart pounded as he neared the porch steps, eyes fixed on the shattered front door hanging off its hinges. He barely registered the rain falling around him, his mind locked on the image of Beretti alone inside.

As Jacobi climbed the steps, he froze, his eyes landing on the hulking form sprawled across the entryway—the Dogman, massive and unmoving. "Holy shit," he muttered, catching his breath as he took in the sight. The creature's amber eyes stared blankly at the ceiling, limbs twisted at unnatural angles, dark blood pooling beneath its head. Even in death, its presence was unsettling.

Just to be sure, Jacobi gave the beast's side a solid kick. A hollow thud echoed through its ribcage, confirming it wasn't getting back up.

He forced himself forward, calling out, "Beretti!" as he stepped inside. His eyes adjusted to the dim interior, sweeping over the room until he spotted her on the kitchen floor, rifle at her side, cradling her arm.

"You okay?" he asked, dropping down beside her. His gaze landed on her arm, where a long, deep gash oozed blood. Frowning in concern, he reached into his vest and pulled out a QuikClot bandage, pressing it firmly against the wound to slow the bleeding.

Beretti gave a faint nod. "I'm alright," she replied, glancing down at her arm. "This isn't from the Dogman—it's from that damn fence." She managed a tired smile, though her face was pale.

"Still deep enough to need a bunch of stitches." Jacobi secured the QuikClot bandage, his voice laced with worry. "I'm calling Perry and getting an ambulance."

Beretti opened her mouth as if to protest, but she relented, her fatigue finally catching up to her. She leaned back against the cabinets, her breathing evening out as she watched him make the call.

Jacobi dialed Perry, keeping a steady hand on Beretti's shoulder as he waited. Perry answered quickly, his tone tense. "Jacobi, what's going on?"

"We got it, Perry. Well, technically Beretti did. The Dogman's down inside a vacant house—don't have the street name," Jacobi said, the relief evident in his voice. "But Beretti's hurt. She needs medical attention."

"Is it bad?" Perry's voice tightened with concern.

"Deep cut on her arm. Can you radio for an EMT as you head over? It's… a scene, to say the least. The house is a block south from where I saw you earlier."

"Will do. And yeah, I know the house you are talking about. On my way," Perry replied, the faint sound of a car engine revving in the background.

He turned back to Beretti, whose breathing had slowed, though her face showed signs of pain.

"Help's coming," he said softly, pressing down on her arm to stop the bleeding. "They'll have you fixed up in no time."

Beretti looked up her eyes landing on the Dogman sprawled lifelessly at the doorway. She exhaled, her voice barely above a whisper. "It's finally dead."

Jacobi followed her gaze, taking in the beast's still form, and nodded. "Yeah, it's over."

They settled into a comfortable silence, the tension of the past few days slowly easing. Jacobi glanced over at Beretti, briefly admiring her strength and level-headedness. Even after everything they'd faced, she remained steady, focused—a grounding presence amidst the chaos.

After a moment, Beretti looked down, then back to Jacobi. "You know, even though I hunt these cryptids, there are times... most of the time, honestly, when I feel a bit of sympathy for them." Her voice softened, and she looked away as she continued, "It's almost always because humans were involved, in some way, in why they went rogue."

Jacobi nodded, acknowledging her point of view. He didn't reply immediately, letting her words linger.

"It's just... I don't know. Seeing them up close like that," she murmured, her gaze returning to the Dogman, "it hits you differently. These creatures are out here, fighting to survive, and somewhere along the way, we intrude, turning them into something they were never meant to be."

Before Jacobi could respond, the distant wail of sirens broke the quiet, and he exhaled, a flicker of relief passing over his face. He glanced toward the open doorway as the lights from Perry's cruiser cut through the rain, illuminating the house in flashes of red and blue.

Stepping onto the porch with wide eyes as he took in the scene, Perry's gaze landed on the Dogman's massive body, and he took a moment to absorb it, a mixture of awe and shock crossing his face.

"Holy… that's it?" Perry asked, his voice barely above a whisper.

"Yep," Jacobi replied, exhaling. "Dead as a doornail thanks to Beretti."

"And you, Jacobi," Beretti corrected.

As the paramedics entered, they came to an abrupt halt, eyes widening as they took in the enormous creature sprawled across the entryway. One of them muttered an astonished "What in God's name?" before quickly pulling themselves together, remembering their task. With a sharp breath, they turned to Beretti, refocusing.

One paramedic knelt down, lifting her arm gently to examine the wound beneath the bandage. "Looks like it's been a rough one," he murmured, unwrapping the gauze and beginning to clean the gash.

Beretti managed a faint smirk, meeting his gaze. "You could say that. Just need a few stitches, and I'll be back in action."

Perry stood nearby, his gaze shifting from the Dogman to Beretti. With a tired smile, she locked eyes with him, feeling the burden of the night fading away.

The paramedics finished dressing her wound, then helped her to her feet, taking a wide berth around the Dogman's body as they guided her out the door. Beretti cast one last look at the creature, a mixture of relief and sadness flickering in her eyes as she took in the hulking figure that had once terrorized the town but now lay still and defeated.

As they guided her to the ambulance, a quiet settled over the scene. The town was safe once more, but the night's events lingered in the cold air—a reminder of the thin line between predator and prey, human and creature, and the balance they had fought hard to restore.

FIFTY-THREE

The following afternoon, the sun cast a golden glow through the sheriff's office windows as Beretti and Jacobi stepped inside. The usual hum of activity filled the room, though a few deputies cast glances their way. Perry, waiting for them by the reception desk, stood up as they approached. His gaze fell to Beretti's bandaged arm, a faint smile tugging at his lips.

"Hey," he greeted them, extending a hand to Jacobi. "Thank you both. Not sure what we'd have done without you." He looked over at Beretti. "I'd shake your hand too, Beretti, but… considering the circumstances."

Beretti smirked, nodding as she held up her bandaged

arm. "I'll take a rain check on that. But we appreciate it, Perry."

Before they could say more, the heavy sound of footsteps echoed through the office as Sheriff Becan entered, his gaze sweeping over the agents with a practiced, managerial nod. He stopped a few feet away, offering a thin, obligatory smile.

"Agents," he greeted, tilting his head in a gesture that bordered on dismissive. "I suppose I owe you a quick thanks for helping take care of that… creature."

Jacobi raised an eyebrow, his expression hardening. "Yeah, 'thanks.' But it seems you were pretty quick to tell the press it was you and your department—with a little help from the FBI—that took down a rogue 'wolf.'"

Becan's eyes narrowed briefly, but he quickly chuckled in a way that didn't quite reach his eyes. "Look, Agent Jacobi, that's the way it goes in small towns. These people—" he paused, gesturing vaguely to the office around him as though "these people" encompassed the entire town, "—need to know their sheriff can take care of things. Keep 'em safe. You FBI folks roll in, handle a case, then you're gone. Meanwhile, I'm still here." He crossed his arms with a slow, deliberate breath. "Besides, I never asked for your help, did I?"

Beretti's eyes flashed with irritation, but she held her

tongue, watching him closely as he continued.

"Don't get me wrong," Becan went on, his voice dripping with self-assurance. "The help was appreciated, of course. But as far as these folks are concerned, I'm the one who keeps this town safe. And that's how it'll stay." His gaze shifted between them, his eyes hard, before he gave a dismissive nod and retreated to his office, the door clicking shut behind him.

Jacobi shook his head, muttering, "Of course, that's how it 'stays.' Can't risk his 'esteemed' reputation by admitting he was in over his head." He glanced over at Perry, who just sighed, looking resigned.

Perry gave them a knowing look, lowering his voice. "Becan's been here a long time, used to getting his way. The town are used to him, but if they knew… I just want you both to know that us deputies know who did the real work here."

Beretti gave him a nod, her expression softening. "Thanks, Perry. It's people like you who actually keep the place running. We see that."

Perry's lips curled into a dry smile. "Still… watching him take credit did stir some annoyance within me. I doubt half the town will believe he did it, though." He shrugged. "But around here, the truth doesn't always reach the people who need to hear it."

Perry extended his hand, shaking Jacobi's again before looking to Beretti. "Well, if you ever find yourselves back in town, you'll know who to reach out to."

But Beretti and Jacobi remained in place, a glint in Beretti's eye as she turned to Perry. "Actually, Perry, there's one more thing we need to do."

Perry raised an eyebrow, curiosity lighting his face. "Oh? What's that?"

Without another word, Beretti and Jacobi turned, heading down the short corridor to the sheriff's office. Jacobi knocked once before pushing open the door. Becan looked up, irritation flashing across his face as they entered.

"Agents," he said, standing from his desk. "If you're here to say goodbye, make it quick. I've got a town to look after."

Beretti took a step forward, her face set, her voice steady. "Sheriff Becan, I need you to stand up."

The sheriff's brow wrinkled, a mocking smile tugging at his lips. "What the hell for?"

Jacobi's voice was cold, unyielding. "You're under arrest."

Becan's face went slack, then he let out a nervous chuckle, shaking his head. "You gotta be freaking kidding me," he said, as if hoping this was all a joke. But the steely resolve in Beretti's gaze told him she wasn't kidding around.

FIFTY-FOUR

The sheriff's indignant shouts echoed down the station hallway as Beretti and Jacobi escorted him, cuffed and fuming, toward the exit. Becan twisted against their hold, his face flushed a deep red, the ever-present vein on his forehead pulsing wildly as he struggled to wrench his arms free. "These cuffs are too tight!" he yelled, his voice loud enough to rattle the windows. "You hear me? I'll have both your jobs for this! Did you forget who I am? I am the sheriff dammit!"

Jacobi smirked, not breaking stride. "Oh, we know exactly who you are," he replied dryly. "A *former* sheriff facing federal charges."

A crowd had gathered outside the station, drawn by an anonymous post on Facebook. As Sheriff Becan was led out in cuffs, the crowd erupted in murmurs and laughter, his face flushing a deep red. The flashing lights of local news cameras captured every detail, reporters jostling for the best shot.

Then, from the back of the crowd, someone yelled, "What's the matter, Bacon? Getting a little crispy?" The crowd broke into laughter, and a smirk even crept onto Jacobi's face.

Becan's head snapped up, face red with fury. "It's Becan! B-E-C-A-N!" he shouted, twisting against the cuffs. But his protests only fueled more laughter, and someone else hollered, "Looks like Bacon's cooked!"

Becan's sputtering turned to more strained protests, but Beretti's grip was firm as they reached the parking lot, where two federal agents waited beside a black SUV, watching with stoic expressions. "You can't do this! Get your hands off me!" Becan demanded, his voice cracking as he threw a final, futile struggle.

"Not a chance, sheriff," Beretti replied, steady and unyielding. "You're right where you should be."

Jacobi opened the SUV door and with a firm shove, they got him inside. He lunged forward as much as the cuffs allowed, shouting, "You think you know everything? You don't know who you're dealing with!"

Beretti leaned in, meeting his furious gaze head-on. "You're being arrested for multiple federal offenses: violating the Endangered Species Act by illegally killing protected wildlife, and trafficking animals in violation of the Lacey Act. We're talking about trafficking endangered wolves, bears, mountain lions—anything you could sell on the black market."

Becan's eyes widened, his bluster fading as the seriousness of his situation started to sink in. But Beretti wasn't done.

"You're also looking at charges for conspiracy to commit wildlife trafficking and violations of the Animal Welfare Act. And because of how you and the Mayor set up this operation, you're being hit with RICO charges for organized crime," she added. "So yes, sheriff, we know exactly who we're dealing with."

Becan slumped back, the color draining from his face. He opened his mouth to argue, but Jacobi cut him off. "Just so you know, agents are already at the Mayor's house. He's under arrest, too. This operation is finished, sheriff."

As Beretti read him his rights, Becan sat in stunned silence, his bravado vanishing with each word. But as the agents finished and shut the SUV door, he began shouting again, his protests muffled as the vehicle pulled away, disappearing down the road.

Jacobi and Beretti watched the vehicle until it was out of sight before turning back toward the station. Perry stood on the steps, flanked by deputies and office staff, all of them watching with wide-eyed disbelief.

As they approached, Perry's eyes narrowed with confusion. "What... just happened?" he asked, looking between Beretti and Jacobi.

Beretti stopped in front of him, meeting his gaze with a firm expression. "After we learned Tucker and Bo were trapping animals illegally, I asked my superior, ASEC Ward, to dig deeper into Becan. We found out he's been running a wildlife trafficking ring for years, and the Mayor was in on it with him. This wasn't just local poaching; they were selling protected species on the black market."

Perry's jaw dropped, a flash of anger and shock in his eyes. "Wildlife trafficking... I had no idea. How did you even think to look into him?"

Becan's open disdain for the FBI had made him stand out. They were used to local law enforcement being wary of outside help, but his hostility was intense, almost blatant—enough to raise their suspicions from the start.

Jacobi stepped in, arms crossed as he shared more. "When we started looking, it didn't take long to find some red flags. Did you know in addition to his house in town, Becan owns a lake house a few counties over and one in Montana? Combined, they're worth a few million each, which is pretty suspicious on a sheriff's salary."

Perry looked up, stunned, as Jacobi continued. "Then there's the Range Rover his wife drives, the private college his two sons attend—all on a sheriff's pay check. And let's not forget, his wife's a stay-at-home mom."

Beretti shook her head. "It's obvious he's been pulling in some serious money from somewhere else, and it isn't good. "With his close ties to the Mayor, it all pointed to something bigger. The Mayor had another guy running things until six months ago, but when that man skipped town, Becan brought in Tucker and Bo to keep the money flowing. They even had people operating in neighboring counties. It was a pretty sophisticated setup."

Perry ran a hand over his face, the realization settling in.

"All this time, he was risking this town's safety for money. I just can't... Well, I guess the real reason he didn't want you guys to come here was the attention it would bring on his activities." He looked back at the stunned deputies, disbelief and anger written across their faces.

Jacobi placed a hand on Perry's shoulder. "Now that he's gone, this department is in your hands, Perry. You're exactly the leader this town needs."

Perry nodded slowly, his face steeling with determination. As he turned to face his deputies and staff, he raised his voice with a quiet authority. "We're going to make sure this town knows the truth. And that it's safe from here on out."

EPILOGUE

Jacobi and Beretti drove toward the airport, the small town shrinking in the rearview mirror along with the secrets they'd finally unearthed. Jacobi leaned back, replaying the events of the past few days—a relentless surge of close calls and last-minute discoveries. There was a feeling of finality now, a sense that they'd finally brought some long-buried truths to the surface.

"Feels like we've been here a month," he muttered, glancing over at Beretti, who was reviewing notes on her phone.

She nodded, giving him a wry smile. "Small towns don't get easier, even with experience. But at least the loose ends are finally tied up."

They both sat in a reflective silence, the weight of their work here settling, knowing the town they left behind would never be quite the same.

As they neared the airport, he finally broke the silence. "You know, Beretti," he said, rubbing his neck, "thinking back on everything... there were more close calls than I'd like to count." He grinned at her. "Especially when you went full ninja on that guy in the parking lot. What *was* that move?"

Beretti chuckled, glancing over at him. "Full ninja? That's what you're calling it?" Her eyes sparkled with amusement. "That was a standing armbar into a hip throw. Standard move when someone twice your size thinks they're invincible."

Jacobi shook his head in disbelief. "Standard move," he repeated, laughing. "I'll have to remember that the next time I'm up against someone that size. You threw him like a rag doll."

"It's all leverage," she replied with a smirk. "Besides, adrenaline works wonders."

Jacobi nodded, gazing out the window as the terminal came into view. "Leverage, huh? That goes for more than just combat." His voice softened. "Still a shock to see what people will do for power or a quick buck. They think they're above it all… untouchable."

Beretti's face grew thoughtful. "I know. For Becan and the Mayor, it was never about protecting anyone but themselves." She glanced at Jacobi. "But it's people like Perry who keep places like this steady. The ones who just do the work."

They pulled up to the terminal, and Jacobi hopped out, grabbing his bag and giving her an appreciative nod. "I'm glad it was you on this one, Beretti."

She smirked back. "Ditto Jacobi. Ditto."

Laughing together, they stepped into the terminal, the familiar bustle of travelers, military personnel, and constant announcements grounding them back in their routine. As they neared the security line, Jacobi glanced over at Beretti with a smirk.

"So, what's next?" he asked.

Beretti's grin widened. "ASIC Ward wants us in Maine. Says there's a situation brewing up there that needs our attention."

Jacobi chuckled, shaking his head. "Never a dull moment."

Beretti shot him a knowing look. "Would you have it any other way?"

"Not a chance," Jacobi chuckled. "Maine, huh? Guess there's no rest for us."

"No rest," Beretti echoed, her eyes glinting as they handed over their IDs. As they moved through security, Jacobi felt a rare moment of closure settle over him. For now, they'd done what they'd come to do. The rest was up to those they'd left behind.

****

Thank you for joining **Special Agent Nicole Beretti** in the first book of her new series! She's tackled plenty of challenges before, but this time she had **Special Agent Noah Jacobi** by her side, bringing his own skills to the table. I'm thrilled you were along for the ride, and I hope you enjoyed the journey.

Here's to many more thrilling cases with Beretti—each one stranger, more dangerous, and unforgettable.

Thank you for reading—catch you in the next *Nicole Beretti Thriller*!

****

ABOUT THE AUTHOR

 Luka T. Jacobs, an author from the picturesque Illawarra region south of Sydney, Australia, is passionate about cryptids like Sasquatch and Dogman. She lives there with her partner and their dog, Finnigan.

Luka's love for animals and adventure fuels her storytelling. With a background in Graphic Design and Art, she adds a unique visual flair to her work. An avid traveler and explorer, she draws inspiration from the wild, eager to share her imaginative worlds with readers.

Luka T. Jacobs

Facebook: https://www.facebook.com/lukatjacobs

Amazon: https://amazon.com/author/lukatjacobs

Website: http://www.LukaTJacobs.com

JOIN CRYPTID HORROR CENTRAL

Join my email list and get first access to new releases and download my **FREE** short story *"The Dogman of Coldwater Creek"*.

WWW.LUKATJACOBS.COM

Dear Reader,

Thank you for choosing my book from so many options. Your support truly means the world to me.

If you enjoyed the story, I'd greatly appreciate it if you could share it with others and leave a review. As a self-published author, your reviews and recommendations are essential in helping me reach more readers.

Thank you again for your support!

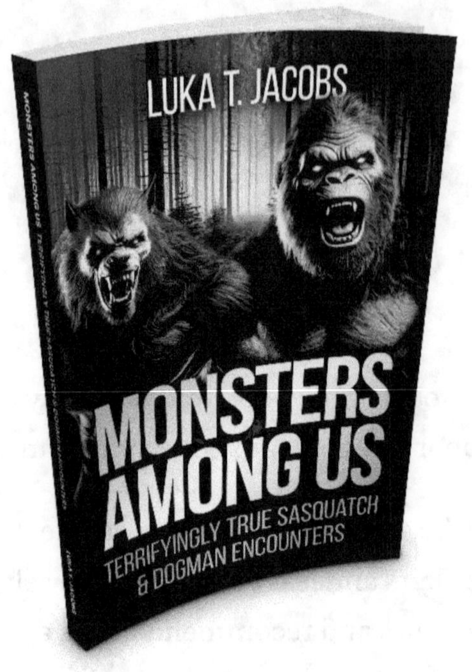

If you're a fan of the eerie and the unsettling, if you crave stories that will keep you awake with every creak and rustle in the dark, then this book is for you. ***"Monsters Among Us"*** is your ticket to the ultimate collection of true, terrifying encounters that will make you question what really lurks in the shadows.

SNEAK PEAK: MONSTERS AMONG US—NIGHT AT THE ROADHOUSE

IDAHO

My name is Huck and I've been a trucker for over twenty years. Born and raised in Idaho, I've driven these roads more times than I can count. I've seen my fair share of weird things out there, but nothing quite like what happened one chilly November night at a roadhouse just off Highway 95.

I was hauling a load of potatoes down to Boise and decided to pull over for the night. The roadhouse was a popular spot for truckers—a small diner with a big parking lot, always a few rigs parked overnight. I found a spot near the back, turned off the engine, and settled in for some much-needed shut-eye.

The night was clear, and the air had a bite to it, a reminder that winter was here. The parking lot was quieter than usual, with only a few other trucks scattered around. I closed my eyes and tried to drift off, but for some reason, sleep wouldn't come. After tossing and turning for what felt like hours, I finally gave up and decided to get out and have a smoke.

I stepped out of the cab and lit up a cigarette, the ember glowing bright in the dark. The night was eerily quiet, not a sound except for the occasional rustle of leaves in the wind. It was spooky, to be honest, like the calm before a storm. I looked around, seeing the dark shapes of the other trucks silhouetted against the dim glow of the roadhouse's neon sign.

Something didn't feel right, but I couldn't put my finger on it. I don't get spooked easily, so I took a deep drag and tried to shake off the unease, chalking it up to being overtired. After a few minutes, I finished my cigarette, flicked the butt away, and climbed back into the truck. I laid back down, hoping sleep would come easier this time.

It couldn't have been more than twenty minutes later when I was jolted awake by a strange noise. It was a scraping sound, like something dragging across metal, followed by a blowing noise, almost like a deer makes. My heart started pounding in my chest, and I strained to listen. The noise stopped for a moment, then started up again, louder this time.

I sat up in my bunk, peering out the window. The parking lot was dark, and I couldn't see much beyond the dim glow of the diner. The noise continued, scraping and blowing, unnerving me. I'd never heard anything like it before.

Out of my peripheral vision I saw movement between the trucks. At first, I thought it was a wolf, but something was seriously off. It was walking on two legs, hunched over, and had hands similar to a raccoons. It's lower body was skinny but the top half looked like it was pure muscle.

I could only see it from the back, but it was enough to make my blood pressure sky rocket. It was slightly hunched as it sniffed the air, then it headed towards another truck parked a few spaces away.

Is that a freakin' werewolf, I thought.

My brain whirled, attempting to process the sight before me. It looked like a wolf, but wolves don't walk on two legs. I watched in horror as it reached the other truck, disappearing into the shadows. The blowing noise came again, louder and more insistent.

I wanted to get out of there, to start the engine and drive away as fast as I could, but I didn't want it to notice me. I couldn't move, couldn't think. All I could do was sit there, heart pounding, eyes fixed on the spot where the creature had disappeared.

I am 55 years old and nothing has ever terrified me like that creature did.

After a while, the noise stopped. The night was silent again, and I tried to calm my breathing. I laid back down, pulling the blanket up to my chin, ears straining for any sound. I don't know how long I lay there, tense and trembling, but eventually, exhaustion took over, and I drifted off to sleep.

I woke up to the harsh light of morning, the events of the night before feeling like a bad dream. But the unease was still there, a lingering sense of dread that wouldn't go away. I climbed out of the truck, looking around the parking lot. Everything seemed normal, but I couldn't shake the feeling that something was watching me.

I quickly did my pre-trip inspection, eager to get back on the road and put as much distance between me and that roadhouse as possible. As I pulled out of the lot, I vowed never to stop there again. Whatever that thing was, I didn't want to see it again.

In the days and weeks that followed, I couldn't stop thinking about that night. I tried to rationalize it, to convince myself that it was just my imagination, that I was overtired and seeing things. But deep down, I knew what I had seen was real. The memory of that creature, walking on two legs, its movements, haunted me.

I dared to mention my sighting to a few other truckers, but most of them just laughed it off, thinking I was joking around. One old-timer though, stopped me as I was leaving and simply said "what you saw was real".

I was a bit taken aback, but glad I wasn't the only one that had seen this evil-looking creature.

SNEAK PEAK: MONSTERS AMONG US—THE FACE UNDER THE PORCH

I've got to tell you a story that's been haunting me for years. My name's Jason, and I'm 26 now, living in Vancouver. I moved here for college, wanting to put some distance between myself and the place where this story takes place. My parents have a rural property outside of Kamloops, BC, and I've hated it ever since we moved there when I was 15. I never could quite explain why—it just never felt right to me. My parents, though, they absolutely love the place.

Recently, I decided it was time for my girlfriend, Emily, to meet my folks. She'd been curious about my reluctance to visit my childhood home and why I seemed uneasy whenever it came up in conversation. I thought maybe facing it head-on would help, so we flew into Kamloops, hired a car, and started the drive out to the property. It was around 7 PM in early May, with the sun just dipping below the horizon.

As we pulled down the long gravel driveway, I felt that familiar knot of unease tighten in my stomach. The driveway was flanked by tall trees on either side, and the house sat at the end like an island of refuge—or, in my case, a place of dread. My parents had installed a motion-operated light on the front porch, but it didn't do much to cut through the encroaching darkness. I even commented to Emily about how useless that light was, trying to mask my nerves with a bit of humor.

We parked and got out of the car. I grabbed Emily's hand, partly for comfort and partly to reassure her. As we walked towards the porch, I stopped suddenly. There was something under the porch, just at the edge of the dim light. I pulled Emily back towards the car quickly, my heart pounding.

"What's wrong?" she asked, her voice tinged with confusion and concern.

"Just get in the car," I said, trying to keep my voice steady.

We climbed back in, and I backed up the driveway, not taking my eyes off the porch.

Once we were a safe distance away, Emily demanded to know what had happened. I took a deep breath and tried to calm down before explaining. "When I got closer to the porch, I saw a face under there. At first, I thought it was just a dog or something, but then it grinned at me—like an evil Joker's grin, all teeth and malice. It was like a wolf's face, but not quite. It had this sinister look in its eyes. It's face was pure evil."

Emily looked at me, her eyes wide. "Are you sure it wasn't just a neighbor's dog or something?"

I shook my head. "No way. It was too large and I have never seen a dog look like that thing before. It is like it wanted me to see it and it wanted me to be terrified. I don't know how I know that, but I do."

I called my parents from the road and told them what I saw. They were angry and brushed it off, insisting it was probably just a neighbor's dog. I wasn't convinced and refused to go back. We agreed to meet in town at a restaurant instead. Over dinner, I tried to convince them to move, but they were adamant about staying.

The rest of the trip was uneventful, but that encounter

refuses to leave my mind. I will never go back to that property.

Emily believed me, and we talked about it here and there, trying to make sense of what I'd seen. To this day, my parents still live there, but I've never set foot on that land again. There's something out there, something that doesn't want me around, and I'm more than happy to oblige.

Monsters Among Us: Terrifyingly True Sasquatch & Dogman Encounters is only available at <u>Amazon for Kindle and Paperback</u>. Get your copy today!

CURRENT TITLES FROM

Luka T. Jacobs

AS AT AUGUST 2024

www.ingramcontent.com/pod-product-compliance
Lightning Source LLC
Chambersburg PA
CBHW072041190726
48294CB00005B/1350

9 781763 780927